THE OUTLAW
of
NAVAHO MOUNTAIN

THE OUTLAW

of

NAVAHO MOUNTAIN

by

ALBERT R. LYMAN

Published by
DESERET BOOK COMPANY
Salt Lake City, Utah
1963

Printed by

DESERET NEWS PRESS

in the United States of America

FOREWORD

Readers familiar with Albert R. Lyman's terrific story-telling ability know that many enjoyable and profitable hours await them in reading *The Outlaw of Navaho Mountain.*

Few writers combine so many of the skills of great writing with such an intimate command of their story material. From beginning to end *The Outlaw of Navaho Mountain* is a fascinating array of high adventure, warm humor, relentless conflict, tender romance, heart-breaking tragedy, and sober truth. Lessons of life are indelibly impressed in unforgettable scenes as we follow the outlaw from cradleboard to rude grave. The many facets of this novel are essentially true.

The ultimate test of a writer's worth is measured by what he gives his readers of lasting value: Does he give them greater understanding? deeper compassion? stronger conviction?

The author of *The Outlaw of Navaho Mountain* does all this and much more.

The Editor

CONTENTS

CHAPTER ONE

SOWAGERIE, WHICH MEANS GREEN-HAIR

A dozen mounted Paiutes followed the winding trail through the dust and the shadscale of the desert south of Clay Hill. In the early twilight of that September day they paused on the bank of the San Juan river to water their thirsty ponies. Then they rode through the low stream to the Navaho country on the other side. West of them, as the shadows deepened, the rugged outline of Navaho Mountain cut off the last glimmer of day, leaving them to follow the dim trail on and on into the night.

"*Pikey—tooish apane!*" (Come on—hurry up!) urged Mike, their leader, a short, thick man with massive neck and ponderous mouth. "Hurry up or the sun will be shining before we get there. Why so slow? Any of you want to go back?"

"*Nene kotch,*" (Not I) swore Chee, his pony's head bunting the tail of Mike's cayuse.

"*Nene kotch,*" echoed ten others with emphasis, and they whipped on with new speed into the darkness.

In spite of their haste, the sun *did* shine before they got there. It blazed triumphantly over the broken profile of the eastern horizon, before the weary riders finally sighted the coveted prize in the valley below them—the prize that had lured them into four days of hard riding from their wickiups near Blue Mountain — four long days and then one torturing night in the old-style Paiute saddle.

With excited whispers they contemplated the prize as it moved along the trail in the canyon. "*Soos, so-use,*

wiuni, piuni, watso-wi-uni, nava-ga-uni, mana-ga-uni,"
they counted up to thirty — thirty fat Navaho horses
— blacks, pintos, buckskins. And then — just coming
into sight—a white snorting stallion carrying a man.

That man! That man on the white stallion! What
about him? Maybe he was Tsabekiss, the big Navaho.
If not, he would be sure to fly at once to Tsabekiss with
the alarm, and the whole country would rise like a
whirlwind.

"Kill 'im!" grunted Mike, the Paiute leader, with
unhesitating finality.

"No!" objected Chee. "Take 'im with us."

"Take 'im with us." echoed the ten others, and Mike
yielded to the majority.

Following a carefully-made plan they rode out one
at a time with wide, fawning smiles to the man on the
white horse. It was Tsa. When he betrayed alarm at
their numbers, they grasped the white stallion's bit
and seized Tsa's hands lest he put up a fight or spring
to the ground and dodge into the rocks.

Brusquely they stripped him of every weapon, even
to the knife on his hip, and ordered him to go with them
and make no noise.

Ten of the Paiutes rounded up the thirty horses
and turned them back up the hills towards the San
Juan. Mike and Chee held Tsa on the white stallion,
and forced him to ride on the heels of the flying band.

Into the clear morning air rose the dust of this
headlong flight. A Navaho shepherd girl saw it and
ran to the hogan of Tsabekiss, the big Navaho. *Tsa*
means rock, *bekiss* means his brother. The big Navaho
was the younger brother of the man taken captive on
the white stallion. Being all but left afoot by this daring
invasion of his remote dominion, and alarmed for the

safety of his brother, Tsabekiss ran to his neighbors
for help and for horses. They took up the deeply cut
trail, with the thieves a full hour ahead.

The big Navaho, Tsabekiss, rode a buckskin mare,
as tough as the greasewood on which she had subsisted
from colthood. Behind him thundered ten other
Navahos in a fury, sworn to rescue Tsa or to avenge his
blood at the cost of their own.

Down the rocky, sidling trail the marauding
Paiutes plunged their lathering band in a mad rush of
hoofs and splatters of blood from feet bruised and torn.
They trod one on another's heels, jostling violently
through narrow passes in feverish haste, with Tsa held
helpless between his two unremitting guards.

Down the same perilous trail the pursuing Navahos
plunged furiously with lash and lather, beating hoofs,
and muttered curses. The stalwart Tsabekiss hurtled
in the lead, his pent wrath fairly hissing between his
teeth, *"Chinde! Cliz bekigie!"* (Devil! Snake-skin!)

"Cliz bekigie!" echoed the ten behind him. With no
horses to drive, they gained steadily on the wild outfit
ahead. Up hill and down with merciless urge, they drew
nearer and nearer till they caught sight of the jostling
band stringing into the mouth of a little canyon not
far ahead.

"Ta-halo!" (Hold!) called Tsabekiss wildly to his
men as he abruptly reined in his yellow mare in terror.
"We are riding into an ambush! We must find a way
out to one side."

A heap of stones in a dry silent region marks the
only place where four states of the United States corner
together. This isolated spot is known as Four Corners.
Walk around this heap and in five seconds you have

traversed a little territory of Utah, Colorado, New Mexico, and Arizona!

In 1860 this wilderness point stood far beyond the wild frontier of civilization. To the northwest of it lay what is now San Juan County, Utah, a rugged, broken area about the size of the state of New Jersey. It was the heritage of a thousand Paiutes, a degenerate off-shoot of the big Ute tribes of Utah and Colorado. Their name stems from the original name *Ute* plus *pi* or *pah* which means water. It originated as a term of reproach to the fathers of the Paiutes for their refusal to join the main tribe in facing the dangers of war on the uplands. Because they stayed in their camps down by the water, they became known contemptuously as Water-Utes or Paiutes.

These Paiutes of San Juan stubbornly refused any ʿgovernment-appointed reservation. Descended from generations of self-willed unconquered ancestors, they insisted on making their own laws with complete dis-regard (if not open scorn) for the requirements of the United States, then a century old. They proved them-selves more than a match for the thousands of Navahos across the river to the south. Having nothing to lose in the way of property, they became merciless parasites on their industrious Navaho neighbors, Besides their su-perior trickery in expeditions of plunder, they could re-treat to their chosen wilderness and disappear among the rocks like rats in a lumberyard. The San Juan River separated the two tribes of this remote region, serving as a barrier of defense between them or as a base of attack in their frequent conflicts.

A dozen soreheads among the Paiutes, chafing because of the way things were divided among the tribe, sulked apart, plotting for a way to better their lot without sharing with the whole Paiute nation. At

length they had incubated a plan to rob the unsuspecting Tsabekiss in his remote valley of the Navaho
country.

In their frantic flight toward the ford of the San
Juan River, Mike and his gang saw Tsabekiss and the
other Navahos hot on their trail. Taking the situation
carefully into account, they dragged Tsa from the back
of his stallion, leaving him to stagger painfully to his
feet, dodge the flying hoofs around him, limp back over
the trail to meet his brother and his baffled tribesmen.
Then the desperate thieves headed into a narrow cleft
toward a high rim. Mike knew that the Navahos would
expect an ambush so he planted none. Instead he rushed
on with his whole outfit for the top.

Tsabekiss and his men knew it could be certain
death to follow the Paiutes up through that cleft. They
also knew that while they hunted a way around, the
robbers could plant some more deadly ambushes far
ahead beyond the river.

"Chinde! Cliz bekigie!" (Devil! Snake-skin!)
shouted the big Navaho to the moving forms he could
discern on the cliff above him. "We'll see you again!"
Seething with determination for future revenge, he
turned his yellow mare and started back with his
helpers the way they came.

Mike, Chee, and the ten other exultant marauders
hurried away to the ford with their choice plunder,
and then onward northeast through the desert shadscale to gloat among their people whose divisions and
decisions they had resented.

Tsabekiss and his friends planned for stern and
immediate reprisal but were thwarted by an unforeseen
fate. Without warning, a division of United States
troops under Kit Carson's command arrived in the ter-

ritory intent on punishing the Navaho nation for repeated breaches of treaty. Although Tsabekiss in his little estate at the foot of the mountain had taken no part in the trouble, yet it had been instigated by his people, and he and his friends were rounded up with thousands of Navahos and driven away to Bosque Redondo—a prison camp near Santa Fe, New Mexico.

The empty Navaho country beckoned loudly to the disgruntled Mike and his gang. With their squaws and papooses, he and Chee and the others broke off from the lawless Paiutes north of the San Juan River and rode away in high dudgeon. Crossing the river with triumphant yell they claimed the estate of Tsabekiss and the isolation its remoteness offered. Here, a hundred and fifty miles west of Four Corners, they could reign supreme at Navaho Mountain, the safest hideout of the entire Southwest. The isolated elevation was made to order for the lawless rebels. They gravitated to the mountain like fleas to a shaggy dog, taking vigorous root in its fertile soil. Big-mouth Mike was still the leading spirit of the deserters, with Chee his chief supporter.

This unusual dovetailing of events stripped the wild elevation of its cumbering Navaho stock, and planted in the place thereof the most lawless faction of the most lawless tribe in the West—the most disgruntled essence of the disgruntled Paiutes. Some strange fate had ordered this cradle of anarchy to bring forth and send abroad a true type of its primeval progeny.

In this way it came about that Chee and his two Paiute squaws propagated, among the twelve deserters in Navaho Mountain, a breed of rebels destined to hold out half a century in rebellion against the settlers in San Juan and in defiance of the government of the United States.

CHAPTER TWO

THE UNTAMED HEIRS

One of Chee's wives was wiry and slender, the other heavy and slow. About the year 1867 they brought forth to their lord two howling little heirs with deep dark eyes and stiff, black hair. Neither the father nor the mothers saw any need of preserving the date of these arrivals. In facts, they had no name nor number for any day or month of the year, and the years themselves passed like idle days with nothing more important than the goad of immediate necessity to motivate action. However, the two little savages were destined in due time to register their own existence in terms sufficiently positive to demand personal attention of the nation's big general at Washington.

Each Mrs. Chee could cinch a torturing saddle on a sore and protesting cayuse, load that saddle with pelts and blankets, and on the top thereof she could arrange sacks and bundles of *ticabba* (food), and quarters of venison to a prodigious height. On each side of this cargo she could hang two or three wicker jugs of water, and lash on a dozen tent poles to drag behind. Astride this ponderous camel-hump she would ride in state with her vociferous infant jolting along in his *cohin* (cradleboard) on her back.

Whatever frisky notion her pony might have entertained, he soon learned to move slowly and carefully under the burden of Mrs. Chee, her household furniture, her groceries and her portable house. She took the most direct course to their next camp-ground, no matter what excursions her lord might choose to take for game or for pleasure. At the new camp she leaned the little *cohin* with its whimpering tenant against a tree or a rock, unloaded the jaded cayuse, put up the wickiup, and prepared refreshments for her tired lord.

Each mother, having no such luxury as diapers for her son, padded his little body with ruffled cedar bark and laced him in his hard cradle-board. From under the rude awning of that cradle-board, her son of promise gazed away, over the pony's tail as they rode, at ridges and canyons destined in the future to give him welcome shelter at intense intervals in his stormy career when the wrath of dishonored law reached angrily after him.

Turned loose to wallow in the dirt long before they were weaned, the two little copper urchins took on a deeper shade of brown. Under the driving sun their hair bleached out into a dirty green. Lord Chee fondled his little cubs, playfully calling one of them *Sowagerie*, which means green-hair. To the other, he gave the name *Beogah.*

Sowagerie, whose real name was Soorowits, was the son of the slender woman. In later years he took the name Posey but that is an English name which had not yet been spoken in the wild mountain. It was a name that one day would arouse mixed fellings of dread and contempt in the hearts of both Indian and white.

The two little cubs, racing the hills with no vestige of clothing to hamper their motion, became quick as squirrels and tough as coyotes. With their crude little bows and arrows they answered the lure of the wilderness, exploring its dens and shooting at its wild creatures or its shadows.

They committed no sins, for nothing was forbidden. No haunting spectre was raised before them of a life too indolent or too unsanitary. They rolled off their sheepskins early in the morning, and hunted and played where they pleased till hunger or weariness brought them back to the wickiup.

They heard no orders to wash their hands and faces, no exhortation to comb their hair, or to put on or take off any article of clothing. They had no books, no lessons, no teachers, no chores, no morals, no commandments. One day was as good as another to them. Every day was a holiday. They howled to it their uncouth good-morning or their irreverent good-night, never dreaming what stern realities this stream of days and nights was to bring.

In the eyes of the ignorant, Old Chee was an ideal father, his wives ideal mothers — not because of any superior methods they had with children, but because they had no method at all. They knew how to mind their own business and refrain from meddling in the natural development of the little boys. By this unusual upbringing, the two brothers were prepared to carry the red banner of Navaho Mountain defiantly against the advancing civilization that already loomed on the horizon. They would maintain their banner's unwritten statutes with a daring and persistency to be admired though not commended.

While the imprisoned Navahos languished in their bullpen near Santa Fe, or hid where they could from the vigilance of Carson's troops, the twelve Paiute deserters ravaged the empty country as far as they had ambition to ride, living fat and reaching more splendid heights of indolence. When the Navaho captives were finally released from their humiliating confinement, reduced and impoverished, the Paiute turncoats, grown insolent and chesty from the abundance they had enjoyed, refused to move a peg in the direction of their own country, even though the pull of want and hunger all around them curtailed at once their standards of living.

The big Navaho, old Tsabekiss, came back from his imprisonment at Santa Fe to find these twelve Paiute parasites and their progeny planted firmly and insolently in the very heart of his estate. They mocked at his threats and his pleadings, compelling him to accept the poor fringe of territory which they allowed. He hated them with vigor for all the hardships his cramped quarters entailed. His brother, Tsa, whom the Paiutes had once captured, had died of tuberculosis in the bull-pen. The strong men who used to be Tsabekiss's ready neighbors were reduced and scattered, leaving him with too few allies to force his will upon the squatters.

The Paiutes returned all his antipathy with interest. Such grudging respect as they gave his limited privileges, was inspired only by the big nation at his back, and by hopes of being able to filch from his industry. If Tsabekiss had been able to fire his destitute people with the full measure of his own indignation, he would have driven these foreigners with severe lashing back to their own side of the river.

The Navahos, so lately whipped and humiliated, and so fearful of attracting unfavorable attention from the big white captains who had permitted them to come back to their beloved country in answer to their pleadings, tolerated this little snarl of Paiutes for the time being, just as busy folks tolerate a nest of hornets which they dread to disturb. The defiant little hornets at the foot of the mountain breathed out awful threats about what their invincible braves north of the river would do to the Navahos if these twelve families were forced back into the crowded regions from which they came.

However helpless Tsabekiss was to inspire his own people with the full degree of his wrath, he did succeed in passing its fury on to his little son, Bitseel. This high-spirited Navaho boy absorbed all his father's animosity for the Paiutes, and generated more animosity of his own. He despised the whole infernal gang at the wickiups.

For the two Chee boys, *Sowageri*e and *Beogah*, Bitseel nursed a ferment with biting acid. Being of his own age they appeared more in his world of fancy than any one else of the enemy camp. Bitseel fought them in his dreams. His intense ambition was to pay them back with double measure for every hardship their people had brought upon his father's house.

The Paiutes gormandized on every stroke of their good fortune with never a thought of the morrow. Inbred indolence impelled them to squander every advantage they gained, sinking always back to their fixed plane of poverty like water to its level.

The Navahos, destitute from their severe captivity, found it necessary, even after all their honest efforts, to steal or to starve. Hemmed off on the north by the hornetlike Paiutes, on the east by Carson and his terrible men, and on the south by tribes too poverty-stricken to pay for despoiling, they saw but one way to ply their old profession as robbers. That one way led across the Colorado River, and across the Kaibab to the Mormon settlements of Southern Utah. So they proceeded to steal from the Mormon settlements, herds of livestock and every useful thing they could carry away in safety.

Neither did they completely overlook the Paiutes as a source of plunder. From those twelve obnoxious Paiute squatters in particular, it was the duty and the pleasure of the Navahos to take everything on which they could lay their itching hands, even though it might be something for which they could make no sensible use. Yet with all their vigilence to hold their own, the Navahos stood at a disadvantage. Thieves though they were by training and by inheritance from many generations, they also loved industry. Since they toiled diligently in any avenue open before them for gain, they always had something to lose and could ill afford to enter a stealing contest with neighbors who had nothing to lose!

In his narrow fringe of anemic territory, Tsabekiss built up a flock of sheep and a band of horses besides realizing substantial returns from the blankets woven by his resourceful squaw.

In their three years of free hand in the country, the little snarl of Paiute invaders should have grown rich, yet for all this unusual opportunity they had nothing to show but a few sorry cayuses and a little flock of loud-smelling goats. They had no gumption to make profitable use of anything. When they saw Tsabekiss thriving on his narrow allowance, they told one another and their children he was enriching himself at their expense. With no more empty territory in which to hunt, and with no neighbors to sleep and be robbed, the renegades grew more impoverished, more ragged, more ravenous. Yet they hung in their poverty to Navaho Mountain, fearing to claim place again among their own people whom they had repudiated by leaving.

Up to this time Sowagerie and Beogah had never once combed their matted locks of sun-faded hair, and no one had seen any reason to do it for them. It was but recently that they had felt some unaccountable necessity for wearing a shirt reaching to their knees instead of to their waist.

The Paiutes of the main tribe on the north found the breach between themselves and the Navahos growing ever wider because of the dozen trouble-breeding rebels who had gone out from them. From opposite sides of the winding San Juan River the two tribes glared at each other in envy, mistrust and avaricious plotting. Into this cauldron of murderous larceny two unsuspecting white men ventured in December 1879.

CHAPTER THREE

BLOOD AND PLUNDER

The bleak winter wind moaned over the mesas and foothills southeast of Navaho Mountain. It whispered with chilly breath in a dozen Paiute wickiups at the base of the cliff, driving the smelly sagebrush smoke back down through the flue and mocking at hunger as it crouched by the dull fire.

Gaunt, miserable horses, humped with cold, gnawed feebly at the dry grass-roots along the hillside. High above them on the perilous ledge of the cliff, a flock of spotted goats ventured onto untrodden shelves in search of browse.

Keen ears harked in the wickiups to the moaning wind outside, harked for a sound other than the wind, a sound more fraught with promise. They listened for the sounds of hoofs—Mike was due to return. Mike, the big-mouthed leader of the renegades. Keen ears marked the sound of those hoofs while they were still distant and dim. Mike had been down to spy on the flocks of Tsabekiss. He hoped he would bring a mutton, but even if he brought a pony with any flesh on its bones, they would have it butchered and hidden from all view before the Navahos could know it.

He was bringing good news! His hoofbeats betrayed it. Thirteen-year-old Sowagerie peered eagerly under the ragged flap at the doorway. Already his father, Old Chee, was outside with several others, impatient to hear the report.

Big-mouthed Mike gesticulated in eager excitement —two white men had come up from Monument Valley to the east. They had crossed the mesa to the hogan of Tsabekiss. They had a good outfit—six spendid horses, new saddles, flour, bacon, sugar. They had money too —they bought corn for their horses from the Navahos. Tsabekiss and his son were following the white men. *"Tooish apane!"* commanded Mike, "or we will lose out!"

Mike's report set the camps afire with eagerness. With crackling speed the Paiutes rushed to the hillside for their lean ponies, cinching them with old saddles, with sheepskins, or simply springing astride the bare and bony backs of the unwilling creatures. Then away they whipped in a jostling tangle down the hill. The squaws and smaller papooses stayed behind.

Sowagerie and Beogah were supposed to stay behind, but these fiery whelps had never yet known law or restraint. They were hardly to be shooed away now from such promise of excitement! They wangled into use two half-broken, awkward colts without saddles or bridles — only rawhide thongs half-hitched in merciless tension to the colts' chins. Off they raced to share in the most extraordinary affair that had ever found its way into their remote world.

Over the hills the ragged cavalcade bolted, hair and blankets fluttering in the wind. Their horses' hoofs plowed the dust or beat the frozen earth as the sun sank toward a blue mist on the horizon. Pintos and buckskins lately humped with cold, now reeked with heat and exertion as they raced down a fork of Lagoona Creek. They overtook Tsabekiss and his son skulking along in a sand wash, but they pretended not to see them and whipped onward over an alkali flat.

When the two white strangers caught sight of an outfit coming in haste behind them, they struck up a desperate gait, hoping to keep out of reach till night should cover them. The big Navaho and his son had been careful to keep out of sight, figuring that their prey, if not alarmed, would camp at the little seep, Clee-betow, and be easy victims in the darkness. Something deep in Tsabekiss' heart recoiled at plotting murder with his son, so he planned to steal the horses while the men slept, and then rob their camp while they hunted for their horses.

Mike, the renegade Paiute, scrupled at nothing. He had in mind a quicker way of doing the job. He would make sure of the prize if ever he reached it, day or night.

Filled with alarm at being pursued, the strangers stopped barely long enough to let their horses drink at Clee-betow, and hurried up the steeps to the east. Reaching the rim of the mesa with its sagebrush prairie, they whipped away into the gathering gloom before Mike and his ravening pack could observe in which direction they had gone.

The Paiutes belabored their panting cayuses up the hill. Behind them came the Navaho and his son, thwarted in their purpose, and hissing "Devil! Snakeskin!" They were still hopeful — by good use of their wits — of being winners in the game.

Night descended on the sagebrush before the two competing outfits reached the top. They bent low over their saddles looking in vain for tracks. They listened. They gazed intently at the distant shadows, hoping to catch a flicker of light. They saw darkness only and heard nothing.

Bitseel and his father, Tsabekiss, kept carefully out of hearing, hoping to get in the lead and race on. They would overtake the white outfit along the trail by which it had come. Tsabekiss and Bitseel knew they had better horses than the Paiutes. They believed they had quicker wits also. Almost surely the white men would turn off somewhere and hide among the rocks.

"Tooish apane!" (Hurry up!) urged Big-Mouth in his guttural idiom, ordering them all, and the Chee boys in particular, to ride without making a noise. They turned off across the mesa, riding on and on in single file for hours without a word. Mike stopped. All his renegade following came to a halt around him. Surely they had passed the white men now. They would wait. Then with the first light of dawn they would cut across the country for tracks.

They watched and listened while the stars moved slowly over them. On this memorable night, Sowagerie and his brother registered deep impressions which were to remain with them through their long and tempestuous careers. Hovering around a little flame in a sheltered place to dodge the December blast, the boys stared with dropped jaws at Mike's surly face. In the dim light they framed ideals which were in due time to make them notorious far and wide.

In the gray December morning the Paiutes scattered to the hilltops, scanning the country. Then they struck a line north and south looking for tracks. They found tracks! The leaders signaled the rest to come see: tracks of six big shod horses going east followed by two small, barefoot ponies.

Off the Paiutes dashed in a jostling knot like wolves on a fresh scent. They must hurry! Maybe the big Navaho had decided to do the job in the Paiute way, and had already gone into hiding with the six big horses, and the flour, the bacon, and sugar. At all events the Paiutes must overtake him or their hard race would be in vain.

Whips and heels forced the empty cayuses to cover five miles at killing speed before they caught sight of their Navaho rival and his son. Apparently the two had been going all night, for their horses staggered with weariness. Up to them and past them rode the eager pack.

"Chinde! Chinde!" (Devil! Devil!) hissed Bitseel in agony of exasperation, but the victors grinned their exultant contempt. Sowagerie ran his tongue at his detested rival as he whipped by after his big-mouthed chief.

From the rim of the mesa the lathering gang sighted the two desperate men at the foot of the high hill eastward below them. The two had stopped to drink and to fill a canteen at the hogan of Hoskaniny. Now they were hurrying on in greatest possible haste toward the monuments.

Big-Mouth and his pack, over-eager to reach the bottom, lashed their ponies into mad leaps down the hill without a break until they came alongside the two strangers. The big Navaho and his son toiled persistently after them, and *Hoskaniny-begay* (son of Hoskaniny) joined with them to see how the mad race would terminate.

Mike, short and stout, with massive neck and ponderous mouth, was the personification of insolence. Never in all his life had he had capacity for anything better than insolence, and that gang of Paiutes followed him as wolves follow the most aggressive wolf in the pack. Close behind that big-mouthed leader as he rode, the Chee boys, tousel-headed and savagely raw in appearance with their sleeveless filthy shirts, gulped down impressions from every word he spoke, from every move he made. With wide-eyed expectation and sagging jaws they followed him for the crowning act in the big drama. What they saw that day wrote itself large in their standards for the years to come.

Big-mouth Mike came alongside Herndon Mitchel, the younger of the two men. Their knees touched as he looked up with a menacing grin. "What are you doing here in this country?" he demanded.

"O, just looking around," Mitchel answered, taking apprehensive account of Mike's designing boldness, and the exhausted condition of the pony he rode.

"Looking for what? What are you trying to steal out of this country?" Big-Mouth pursued.

"Nothing," replied Mitchel. Then he thought of the valuable samples in his panniers—samples of silver ore for which John Myric, the older man had induced him to come to the perils of the reservation to act as an interpreter.

Mike looked at him deliberately out of muddy, mean eyes. Slowly and hatefully he grunted, "You lie! You are here to steal silver from the *Peshleki* (the famous Navaho silver mine). You have your big horses loaded with silver."

"You can have all those rocks," said the boy hurriedly, at a loss for a better answer, and depreciating the valued specimens they had come so far and hazarded so much to get.

"Your horses have been eating up our little bit of grass and drinking up our little bit of water," Mike went on in menacing tones of unrelenting purpose.

"There is no grass. We buy our corn for our horses."

"You paid the Navahos money for the corn. Now pay me for the water. I want a hundred dollars for the water these big horses have been drinking."

Herndon Mitchel eyed him in astonishment — the great coarse mouth with its two long rows of devouring teeth, the uncompromising insolence of the demand. He hesitated for an answer.

"Give me a chew of tobacco," ordered Big-Mouth, his grin seeming to soften as if he were about to turn the whole matter off as a joke, for he could see the outline of the square end of a plug in Mitchel's hip pocket.

The half-naked Chee boys with two others of the gang watched Mike with their jaws sagging in expectation. Some of the other Paiutes held the attention of Myric, the older of the two men, pretending to have a great deal to say. The three Navahos, Tsabekiss, his son, and the son of Hoskaniny, followed near enough behind to watch the whole procedure.

Mitchel took Mike's order for tobacco, along with the deceiving grin, to be a friendly rift in the dark clouds. Leaning forward in the saddle, he thrust his right hand into his pocket for that square end of a plug. It was far down and hard to get. He writhed himself into a defenseless posture with his right hand too much engaged for any quick action. That was exactly what Mike had anticipated and planned for. Quick with premeditated skill he snatched Mitchel's pistol from its holster and shot him through the head.

Turning sharply at the sound of the pistol, Myric saw his companion lolling in the saddle. Striking spurs to his weary horse he tried to make a quick dash over the hill. It was a hopeless effort. Before he got his jaded animal into action, Mike fired at him and he rode away with an ugly wound.

As Mitchel fell to the ground, part of the gang stopped his horse and caught the four pack horses, determined to seize upon every valuable their big

"haul" promised. Others bent over the dying Mitchel
on the sand, despoiling him of everything their rapacity
desired, while the rest of the murderous lot chased
after Myric lest he escape with his horse and saddle and
possibly, though that was a remote concern, become a
witness against them.

From the top of the hill they sent more bullets after
the fleeing white man. He returned their fire as he
rode, even though he could see none of them over the
summit. For four miles he held in agony to the saddle,
keeping his pursuers from coming out in sight. Then
he turned over among the rocks of the butte which still
bears his name. The ravenous pack of parasites found
him there—whether still alive no one knows. They
gathered like starving vultures around him, stripping
him to the skin.

Tsabekiss and his son got nothing. They viewed
the naked and blood-soaked bodies of the two men.
Their only emotion was increased hatred for the rivals,
the Paiute renegades who had beaten them to the sport.

The victors returned with their plunder in glorious
triumph to the wickiups at the base of the cliffs by
Navaho Mountain. For three days they reveled in the
most extravagant style the quantity of their loot
afforded. Then to the bedrock plane of their groveling
poverty they lapsed once more. Yet they gloated a long
time over the glorious deed and the easy gain. It was
an inspiring tale to preserve for generations of papooses yet unborn.

A month later, when fourteen white men came
hunting their dead, the Navahos told them who had
done the murder, and led them to the scavenger-picked
skeletons. The twelve Paiute renegades insisted with
equal firmness that the killing had been done by the

Navahos. The whites gave up the investigation and no one was ever made to answer to the law for this cold-blooded murder. That is what made it a cherished memory in the wickiups. That is what made it, in the minds of Chee's sons, a safe feat of heroism. But the gain and glory of it failed to compensate for the degree to which it rendered the intruders more obnoxious to their jealous Navaho neighbors. It began to be difficult and dangerous for the Paiutes to stay at Navaho Mountain.

CHAPTER FOUR

SOWAGERIE AND BITSEEL

A dreary succession of bleak days festered dis-
content among the idle Paiute squatters at Navaho
Mountain. Just when their relations with their Navaho
antagonists had reached the breaking point, exciting
news began sifting into the territory. A company of
twenty-five Mormon scouts had come under the
direction of Captain Silas S. Smith to select a site for
a new Mormon colony. The place they had selected
was a remote point near the San Juan River, fifty
miles from Four Corners and over a hundred miles
from Navaho Mountain. It seemed that the Mormon
leaders had reached this strange decision—planting a
town in the midst of hostile enemies—as a last attempt
to solve the ever-increasing dangers of Navaho and
Paiute lawlessness. Since they had been successful in
winning the friendship of their Indian neighbors elsewhere, they felt confident they could win over the
Navahos and Paiutes in time. It would be a dangerous
move but something had to be done. Only a few months
had passed since the Navahos had murdered one of
their peace envoys with his own gun and caused his
companions to flee for their lives. If the situation were
left unchecked it could soon blaze out of control.

News of this daring peace colony fell on welcome
ears on every side. For over thirty years, the Navahos
and Paiutes had found the white man easy prey,
yielding rich spoil. What could be more convenient than
having a colony of them right in their midst! It would
no longer be necessary to make distant raids to strip the
hills of sheep, cattle, and horses. They would have stock

in their own territory! Well they knew the Mormon
policy to feed Indians rather than fight them. The
Mormons would be ideal neighbors to have!

When the little colony finally arrived after what
seemed endless months to the Paiutes, all the curious
and hostile elements from both tribes came at once
to see it. There it was—a rude log fort with a few
houses going up nearby. The new settlement, called
Bluff, was virtually defenseless before the thousands
of impoverished Navahos just across the river to the
south, and the beggarly hordes of thieving Paiutes on
every other side.

To the indolent Paiute gang at Navaho Mountain,
Bluff offered escape from a bitter tangle with their
Navaho enemies. Without delay they loaded their
poverty onto their cayuses and pitched out for Bluff.
What couldn't be tied on or dragged behind was abandoned. The move was to be permanent if they liked the
prospect. The squaws with their squalling papooses
rode on the huge camel humps of greasy paraphernalia
like royal passengers. At last they reached their des-
tination.

They liked the prospect immensely! They opened
wide their thieving Paiute eyes on the strange little
settlement. They liked the sight of horses and cattle
loose on the hills. They liked the looks of the vegetable
gardens and corn fields. They coveted the valuables left
so often within easy reach. Not since the imprisonment
of the Navahos at Bosque Redondo had the Paiutes seen
so promising a prospect.

In making the move back to the north side of the
river the Paiute gang were braving the contempt and
possible revenge of the main Paiute tribe, whom they
had offended by their original departure. Yet this

hazard, along with the trouble of pulling up stakes and making the long journey, was more than compensated for. It meant getting away from their thorny Navaho adversaries, Tsabekiss and his vengeful son, Bitseel as well as opening new fields of plunder.

Get away from Tsabekiss and Bitseel? this hope was soon blasted. One morning, as the ragshag Sowagerie came from between two houses in the little Mormon fort, he heard a painfully familiar voice. *"Chinde! Cliz! Cliz!"* (Devil! Snake! Snake!) it hissed spitefully. There stood Bitseel drawn up to the full height of his youthful contempt!

Sowagerie drew back in startled fury, viewing his enemy with surprise. Bitseel wore a velvet shirt with a ruffle on the tail. His hair was carefully bound in a bob and held down with a red turban. He had neat moccasins, white factory trousers open on the side up to his knees. Altogether he looked thrifty and of some consequence. Sowagerie, his hair in taglocks and tangles, and his grimy shirt hanging in rags at his knees, felt the contrast of their appearance as the weight behind his enemy's curse.

Bitseel looked him over with haughty disdain. Sowagerie answered by distorting his unwashed face and thrusting forth his tongue snake-like as his best way of making known the feelings which a snake has no words to express. The feud was in their blood-stream. Bitseel had left his home and his father and had come to live with his uncle that he might continue to goad, taunt, torment and hate his enemy at every turn.

Sowagerie's chagrin at this unexpected turn of events was a slight but not unbearable blight on his new way of life. Other wise it was quite satisfactory in every respect. It brought to his dull diet welcome fresh beef at frequent intervals. It put horses of the settlement in easy reach, for since there was little hay or feed, the horses were left loose on the grass whenever they were not in use. While some of the Paiutes begged from door to door, keeping a sharp lookout always for anything of value on which to put their sly hands, they could at the same time ascertain who was at home and who was away, and how safe it was for their gang to plunder the near-by hills.

Sowagerie's people merged again with their tribe, but there followed them a stigma not easy to live down. At the time of their return, old Norgwinup, a patriarch, a dignified old leader of the thousand Paiutes who accepted tribal rulings and stayed together, rehearsed to his people with hateful accusations how these turncoats had gone away. Green-hair felt the sting of their discrimination wherever he went among them. All the same, their ways charmed him. Theirs were the ways of a nation. His were too much the customs of a family. They had numbers, dash, daring, and leading spirits.

And they all played *ducki* (cards), even the squaws! The charm of the game was simply irresistible. The enameled faces of those spot-cards in cooncan and monte (Spanish card games), had a magic lure for Sowagerie from the first day he saw them. Ducki was the gallant game for the big chiefs, whether they won or whether they lost. In it they proved their greatness of calibre, not only by how much they won, but by the game indifference with which they lost. They won big pockets-full of money, so Chee's boy imagined, and they got it in royal style for nothing but the exercise of their wits. They won it from Navahos, from Mexicans, and from one another. The little fellows played for matches or cartridges. The big cavaliers played for silver, blankets, buckskins, guns, hats, knives, horses — anything!

The hostility smoldering between Sowagerie and Bitseel brought the two sufficiently close to each other at frequent intervals to exchange ardent tokens of animosity. Often when a circle of men sat crosslegged around a blanket absorbed in a big game of *ducki*, and Chee's son stood watching them intently, anxious by all means to master the smart tricks of the winning player, he heard his dearest enemy hiss from the other side, and he returned the compliment in kind.

It was inevitable that these two haters should battle in this *ducki* arena. Green-hair's most cherished ambition was to trim the haughty Navaho of all his fine toggery. The Navaho's ambition was to grind his enemy to even deeper humiliation. Bitseel got ready first to make his challenge which he did one day by shaking a deck of cards at his adversary instead of hissing his futile curse. With grim determination Sowagerie accepted the challenge.

They began to play—these young implacables — a game without a single tinge of friendliness or trace of toleration. To these uncompromising enemies the contest promised a new vent for an old grudge long festering. In mistrustful preliminary, without a word, they finished three games with matches only. They threw the cards with all the banter and affront they had seen in the big games, but the trifling matches only mocked at the strong blows each one wanted to deliver.

The Navaho took a silver bracelet from his wrist. "*Hacoon!*" (Come on!) he challenged, holding it up to be matched with something of similar value.

The Paiute had a sleeveless shirt of unknown color, the remnant of what used to be a pair of overalls, and a butcher knife which he had pilfered from the fort. Nothing else. That knife was about his first valuable possession. He had made a crude scabbard in which he carried it proudly on his hip. He hesitated. What if Bitseel should scorn it as too cheap a match for the bracelet? Worse still, what if the Navajo should win it?

"Hacoon!" (Come on!) urged Bitseel, taking quick stock of the situation. He would accept that knife against his bracelet. In fact , the knife was all that justified Bitseel in bantering this penniless beggar to play.

Sowagerie laid the knife alongside the bracelet, viewing the two objects hopefully while he manipulated the cards as if his vigilance would make them both his own. His suspense was short. A flip of the cards made his adversary the winner. Bitseel took the bracelet and knife over with a victorious grin. At the same time he gathered up his cards, for he saw nothing more for which to play, unless it were the shirt of doubtful color, or the vestiges of old overalls. Nothing more, unless it were that ugly scabbard. When he had replaced the bracelet on his wrist he became sociable enough to say, "Give me that scabbard. You don't need it."

"I'll burn it," snarled the Paiute as he turned to go.

Whenever an Indian recovered from a fit of *ducki* becoming conscious of the fact that he had nothing left but his G-string, his quickest way to a new start was to hunt up and sell one or two horses belonging to the Mormon settlement. In that way many a gambler made his first, second and third start. Moreover, the Indians lived on Mormon beef with such unfailing regularity that the people of the struggling colony lacked little of being left afoot and penniless. As a lamb between two wolves the helpless colony was about to be devoured.

These colonists, selected and sent by their leaders to win the confidence and good will of the Indians, fortunately had been provided with one of the best Indian diplomats the frontier ever produced. He knew the Navahos better than they knew themselves, and he spoke the barebarous Paiute dialect so perfectly that you fancied you smelled the wickiups and burning sagebrush whenever you heard him talking to the Indians. That was Thales Haskel.

The Indians were awed by Haskel's piercing black eyes, silvery hair, and white beard. His eyes could penetrate their very thoughts. He was a mystery man. He had the rare ability to keep quiet in four languages. In spite of his consummate mastery of their speech, he used but few well-chosen words to either tribe. That, more than any other one quality, proved that he knew much, for he said little. He would sit unmoved like an image through their long-winded queries and accusations, never betraying the least interest, nor making any sound except to grunt his perfect under-standing of everything they said. Neither did he look at them while they talked, but he frowned studiously down his nose and waited till the situation became fully ripe for the thought he had matured and focused in the most laconic expressions. Then he would turn his black eyes straight into theirs, giving them a thrill as if a lion had awakened from sleep.

"We came here to be your friends," he declared, staring them out of countenance. "Our big chief sent us to sit down by you and help you. You see us toiling here from dawn to dusk and you come sneaking in like a lot of coyotes and steal us blind."

They could not miss the force of his words, and a few of them became his firm friends from the first. Paiute Henry, a slender youth about the age of So-wagerie, was one to declare his love for Haskel and Haskel's people. Through fifty years of change and hardship he proved his fidelity in every crisis. The tribe had a few other men of Paiute Henry's calibre.

Most of the Paiutes mocked at Haskel's words: Sanop and his two boys, Big-mouth Mike, Tuvagutts, Paiute Bob, and the two Grasshoppers. Hatch, one of Norgwinups four sons, sneered his contempt. The other three, Poke, Bishop, and Teegre, took no notice. Old Chee, of the twelve deserters, was favorable, but his two ragtag sons, Sowagerie and Beogah, with their witch-locks of dirty green hair, had taken Poke for their ideal. Whatever Poke said was right.

Poke, the third son of Norgwinup, was the dashing cavalier, the born prince of the tribe. He feared nothing. Everybody feared him—even the members of his father's household. He wore a formidable mustache bristling straight and emphatically down across his mouth, and he wore an extra wide hat with a high crown. He was a dread and imposing figure. Ten years older than the Chee boys, he regarded them as the contemptible spawn of renegades. For this very reason the adoring Sowagerie was eager to worship at his feet.

CHAPTER FIVE

THE GLORIOUS VICTORIES

Whether in response to Haskel's appeal or for reasons of their own, the Paiutes let the settlement at Bluff have a rest while they sought bigger plunder elsewhere. They wanted something more thrilling, something on a grander scale than was possible with the poverty-stricken little colony. And they wanted somebody ready to fight instead of talking peace all the time.

At the Blue Mountain, fifty miles north of Bluff, two big cow outfits had moved in from Colorado, and thirty miles east of the mountain a man named Thurman had located at Paiute Spring with a big band of blooded horses. No greater attraction than those fine horses could have been dangled before the eyes of these restless, thieving Paiutes. They turned their eyes in that direction by instinct as soon as they went from Bluff.

Without comment, or apparent plan, they headed in a long straggling procession for Paiute Spring. Of course they had with them their goats, their household, and all their vociferous offspring. Poke rode in the lead of the big procession. Sowagerie, now in his mid-teens, kept as near to Poke's heels as he dared to ride.

Just as the Paiutes arrived at the springs from the southwest, a horse-buyer named Smith, and May, a companion, arrived from Colorado to buy Thurman's horses, or some of them. Since they came with a first-class outfit, they instantly became as big an attraction to the Paiutes as Thurman's prize band of horses at the ranch.

Checks were not yet the style in San Juan, so Smith had come loaded with silver and greenbacks prepared to pay cash for whatever he purchased. On top of all this temptation, Smith bought a pony from the Paiutes and paid for it in cash. The greedy Paiutes began to form a most daring notion of the almost limitless possibilities before them.

It was a bright morning in April, 1881. The three white men, even though they were alone among Indians in this remote wilderness, saw nothing in the situation to justify any alarm and went on with the business of their intended transaction. The Indians stood innocently around, gaping with curious eyes and talking in their incomprehensible tongue as at other times. They looked harmless enough, with their squaws and papooses trailing after them in family groups—hardly a picture to fill one with fear. Thurman had seen them before and found them apparently inoffensive. He allayed all the mistrust which his visitors might otherwise have entertained, yet cold dread would have seized all three men if they had been able to grasp the import of the dove-tongue babble around them.

Without warning, a volley of shots tore into Thurman's cabin home. The owner fell dead where he stood in front of his doorway. A rod away, the man May fell, to be finished off in savage style. The bullet intended for the horse-buyer, Smith, went wild of its mark and he dodged into a thicket of brush and trees and ran at break-neck speed down the canyon.

Over rocks and ledges Smith made his way in desperate haste, but the pursuit on horses was simply

.fun, and the Indians left him dead behind a great
rock a mile away where his bones lay forty years
before any white man found them.

The Paiutes rifled the dead men's pockets and
stripped them of their blood-stained clothing. They
ransacked the panniers and the war-bags of Smith
and May. They rummaged with ruthless hands through
everything in the cabin, hunting trinkets, money, or
any curious thing in box or trunk. They saved every
bit of paper which looked like money, some if it being
of no value at all. They cut the long straps from three
sets of harnesses and carried away six work bridles
from which they cut off the blinkers.

Glutted and stuffed with whatever appealed to
their ravenous appetites or to their depraved fancy,
they set fire to everything that would burn — the
cabins, the sheds, the wagons, the fences. Having set
the red flame to work all over the scene of their murder
and robbery, they proceeded with their goats, their
new stock of horses, their noisy progeny and all their
hodge-podge of plunder back to the southwest. It mattered nothing that they stirred up a big dust or that
their snarl of family groups made a loud din as they
rode. It mattered nothing that they moved only three
miles an hour. There was no need for excitement or
haste. It would be days or weeks before any posse could
collect to follow them, and if one or two stragglers
should be foolish enough to give chase, that would
but add to their fun and their booty.

On the sandhills four miles north of Bluff, Joe
Nielson was guarding the Bluff horses when late in
the afternoon he saw this long string of Paiutes approaching with their big band of horses. Some of their
gang came out and gathered his fifteen or twenty
head into their big band, and sent a bullet whistling

over his head as an invitation for him to keep out of the way.

They camped that night near Boiling Spring in the valley of the Butler. There, in case of attack, they could vanish from sight into holes and caves and little box canyons on every side. Any army foolhardy enough to try to dig them out, would melt away like a snowball in the flaming hereafter. The glitter of their huge achievement and the charm of their rich plunder, like the suck of a great sponge, had drawn in nearly all the stragglers of the tribe. They glutted and danced and chanted their wild exultation around a circle of fires on the hillside.

In the gray dawn they discovered ten men on the east side of the valley — ten men from Bluff who rode boldly into the big herd of horses scattered in the bottom of the valley and claimed the horses taken from Joe Nielson the day before. Vain of their numbers and greedy of gain, a tangle of angry Paiutes swarmed down from the hillside in ugly objection to anything being taken from their big roundup. The men from the fort, desperate with poverty, held to their own with grim resolution. When the Indians drew their guns, the Mormons countered the movement in readiness to make any killing a mutual affair. It needed only a split second to set off the explosion, and it would be finished in a minute, even if each white man made a kill before he was finished off.

One Paiute, Old Baldy, held a triggerless revolver against Lem Redd's stomach, and was ready to discharge it by hitting the hammer with a stone. Lem Redd had his pistol ready to blow Old Baldy's brains out before he could bring that stone into action. Jess Smith and Amasa Barton each faced ugly rifle muzzles from which death could belch forth at the pressure of an Indian's finger, and each one of them held his own weapon ready to do as much execution as time would permit after the start had been made.

In this thin, throbbing interval, with pandemonium threatening to drop with a bang, the Paiute, Henry, appeared on a high rock above his people and pierced the morning air with a long shrill yell. *"Too itch tickaboo!"* he called at the top of his voice, "These men are our friends—don't hurt them—give them their horses!"

The Paiutes lowered their guns at once. The few who still claimed horses belonging to the people of the fort, were compelled by their own people to yield. Henry was no chief, but moral courage is kingly among men. By his own great soul and the conviction which Haskel had planted therein, he was able to appeal to those same latent virtues in the hearts of his tribesmen.

It was but for a minute, yet a new force had restrained these wild men of the hills. Nothing like it had ever happened before in their history. Sowagerie observed it with disappointment. He wondered why, with all their glory, their superior numbers, and their hands full of loot, they should yield to these few inconsequential men of the fort.

One of the Indians, lousy with his money from the bodies of the dead, gave twenty-five dollars in bills to Jess Smith for a wide hat. Another gave sixty for a similar hat, while others offered in trade, paper which was not money at all. It was plain that the Paiutes had made a raid somewhere, but the news of what had happened at Paiute Springs was slow to reach the fort.

Henry's surprising influence was but the psychological blow at a white-hot moment, a force to which the wild men were not yet disciplined to yield for many seconds at a time. Even if all the old patriarchs of the tribe had backed Henry's sentiments, they would have been helpless to stop that riotous gang from hunting new ways for doing mischief that day as they moved up the Valley of the Butler. Ahead of them, northward, loomed the cliffs of their sure defense. They were anticipating the wondrous occasion when their pursuers would come there to attack them. With all this sure program of exultation in store, why bow now to white man's detested laws and standards?

On the very pinnacle of their triumph they had meekly surrendered a string of valuable horses to the people of the defenseless fort. What squaws they had been! They would compensate to themselves for the loss of the Mormon horses by doing everything they could think of to the Mormon cattle in the valley above them. So they shot down cows, just to see them fall, leaving most of the carcasses to rot untouched. They lassoed calves and cut off their ears on a level with their heads and their tails almost to the hip bones. The more aimless the destruction the better.

They raced madly up and down the country on Thurman's blooded horses, distressed for nothing except lack of quicker and more senseless ways to dissipate their loot and indulge their unusual fortune. At night they gormandized again on the choicest cuts of the finest beef on the range, chanting and shouting as men made drunk by too much spoil.

West of Bulter stretched an impregnable maze of defenses in which, if occasion demanded, they could defy the whole world. That is, all the world they knew or could imagine. Through precipitous territory to the west ran an ancient trail over which their fathers had fled in safety from all pursuit. On that trail they hurled back or destroyed every man who undertook to follow them. In the deep heart of that maze was the mysterious *Pagahrit,* or Standing-water, the sanctuary of absolute safety where at intervals through the years, they chanted to *Shin-op* (God) their praise and exultation.

But they would not go now to their impregnable defenses—they were not that hard pressed. So far this was just a wild lark from which they did not want to run away. The victory trail with its secret places of grass and water was a sacred thing to be reserved for grave emergencies. They would live fat on the outside while they could.

Without hurry or fear they followed dim trails known only to themselves, crossing a broken region into the heart of Elk Mountain where white men had not yet set a defiling foot. Here they awaited their pursuers, certain that they would be on their tracks as soon as their work at Thurman's ranch had become known. While they waited, they danced and chanted their defiance in wild exultation. Their voices echoed away in the midnight through dark groves of aspen and pine.

No enemy came. From the headlong rims of the mountain the Indians gazed hopefully at the haze in the distant east, scrutinizing each smoke and shape where white men's herds had begun like a plague of grasshoppers to eat up the country. Half a moon they watched. No enemy appeared. The enemy was slow and uninteresting.

So, from their place of waiting, in eagerness to play the big game, they sent spies to skulk undercover or in the darkness, to ascertain what was going to be done, if anything, and whether it would be fun to hide any longer. These scouts reported that Uncle

Sam's blue-coated fighters had come as far as Blue Mountain, only to lose courage at that point and return to their fort in Colorado.

Several days after the massacre at Paiute Springs, two cowboys had happened down that way and found the ranch in ashes, the bodies of Thurman and May putrifying in the dooryard, and the man, Smith, missing altogether. They spurred out of there with the alarm. The gruesome news spread like fire in the grass. Indignation mounted to fever heat. Cowmen and friends gathered in a rush and induced a company of soldiers from Ft. Lewis, Colorado, to go with them.

Cowboys and soldiers generally agree like oil and water, and this mixed company was no exception to the rule. They quarreled all the way to Blue Mountain. At that point the soldiers who had volunteered to go along quit in disgust and returned to their barracks, leaving the cowboys to do the job in their own way.

Delay and uncertainty held sway in the Blue Mountain camp. Without organization or discipline they wrangled over a plan on which to proceed. They contended about who should carry the honor of leadership. They disagreed about this phase of the situation and that. No one had the remotest notion as to where the Paiutes could be found — they had disappeared from the known area of the country. Some of the cowboys continued to watch for tracks. Days dragged on into June with no solution of the matter in sight.

CHAPTER SIX

THE LITTLE SISTER

That snarl of tossing, sleepless Paiutes could not abide the uncertainty of waiting there in their hideout all summer. When they received the dull information that Uncle Sam's soldiers had turned back from a point forty miles away, they relaxed in disappointment. Breaking the monotony of their fruitless vigil they headed off to hunt for deer on North Elk and drifted on down into Indian Creek.

June had come, green and inviting. Two months had passed since the big thrill at the springs. So far no avenging hand had found energy or courage to reach after them. They regarded the horse-ranch affair as a closed incident. So from Indian Creek they extended their hunt towards La Sal Mountain. With all their spoil and plunder, their yiping dogs, and their well-fed posterity, they crossed Dry Valley in a motley caravan. In the big open country they saw neither horsemen nor tracks to disturb their composure. Secure and unafraid they camped by a clear stream in a shady canyon of La Sal Mountain, feeling that the mountain was their very own as it used to be before the time of white invaders.

When their straggling procession crossed Dry Valley, it had no more than gone out of sight over a sand-ridge, when a cowboy scout found the hot trail behind them. He bent but for a second over the reeking tracks of their well-beaten trail. Then he tore off over the prairie to spread the welcome word at the Blue Mountain camp. The report came out to that fidgeting center as water to men in the desert. In hot haste they mounted and galloped down over Peter's Hill like a mob of schoolboys at recess time.

Into the harmless din of the new camp in the mountain dell, the clatter of hoofs, the roar of rough-riding cavalry broke on Paiute ears like a bolt from heaven. Wild consternation flew through the wickiups. When the Indians saw that fury of wide hats, flying manes, and drawn guns appear on the hill above them they simply jumped with shrieks of terror and surprise. With their frantic children they stampeded one over another, upsetting wickiups and scattering camp furniture right and left in their eagerness to reach the brush and the rocks. They fled afoot, leaving 'their horses behind. In fact, they left everything behind except their children and their guns.

Afoot! Nothing to eat! No beds, no shelter. They would have to hide like so many coyotes — they who so recently had been glutted and mounted and surfeit with money! They glanced hurriedly back to see the dashing cavalcade envelop the camp, taking horses and everything.

Intoxicated with their tremendous advantage and burning with a desire for revenge, the cowboys leaped from their saddles and ran with their guns after the fugitives. They wanted to exterminate the whole infernal tribe before the Paiutes could get away. Every cowboy, greedy for his full share of the exterminating, left his horse to stand with dropped reins till the slaughter was through.

From a deep thicket of birch willows, Poke called loudly in his incomprehensible language, telling his people to follow up the brush-grown ravine and collect by a big rock they could see above. He told them not to shoot till he gave the signal.

Through tangles of serviceberry the white men crashed stamping over the rocks with their heavy boots and calling recklessly one to another. They shot at every real or imaginary disturbance in the jungle and otherwise advertized their presence wherever they went. Finding their fire not returned they felt the more secure and plunged forward after the enemy.

Once out of sight, the Indians made little noise. In spite of their desperate haste they trod softly and spoke in whispers. At the foot of the big rock up the brushy ravine, Poke waited to direct them over a little ridge, and then down another ravine to a jumble of big rocks.

When he gave the signal to shoot, he led off by killing three white men in three shots. The sudden fusillade surprised the cowboys as much as their own coming had surprised the Paiutes. The whites scrambled for cover, leaving their dead and wounded behind. In a panic they retreated headlong into the wild mountain while Poke and his people, having run a circle, rushed back to their wickiups. They seized everything they had left behind, and along with it they seized the saddled horses, the pack horses, and the complete outfit of the men who had attacked them. Of that formidable company of riders who got away alive, not one saved more than his gun. The Paiutes took everything.

Securing their new gain in the fewest minutes possible, Poke and his people took stock of themselves and their position for defense from further attack. They had more than twice the outfit they had before, and they had lost but one man. They had sent their enemies ignominiously away afoot with their wounded, without food to eat or blankets to rest on. Everything brought by the posse with their blare of trumpets was added to the Paiute horde! Surely *Shin-op* had been fighting for them.

With their enemies in full retreat clear out of the country, the Paiutes went in the evening and dragged twelve dead white men down out of the brush to strip them of all their valuables and leave them carelessly in a row to the crows and coyotes. Besides that, two of Poke's gang had found two unsuspecting prospectors and raised the number of their kill to fourteen. This was seventeen white men killed since the brave start at Paiute Springs in April, and possible more of the cowboys would die, for many of them were badly wounded.

To the worshipful Sowagerie — worshipping unacknowledged at Poke's active heels—the drama from the horse-ranch to La Sal was one continuous vision of glory. Nothing in his short life could ever begin to compare with it. The brightest points in Sowagerie's memory of excitement at Navaho Mountain faded to dimness in comparison. Compared to Poke, Big-mouth Mike seemed like a tame old squaw.

But that tremendous affair at La Sal left another and a very different tingle in Sowagerie's wild being. When the camp had bolted for the rocks, clinging to and stumbling over one another, the weak to the strong and the timid to the brave, a soft hand had reached his own and held firmly till they reached shelter. The grip of any such hand in just that way would have set his heart to beating in higher gear, but this—this was the hand of Toorah, the little sister of Poke, the Paiute cavalier. She had clung to So-wagerie's hand with the startled alarm which had seized everybody in camp. He had wished they might get separated from the tribe and run on and on forever. When she heard her brother's commanding voice, she had smiled her friendly embarassment and, releasing her hold, had hurried with the others toward the big rock up the ravine.

That meeting struck new flame in the heart of Sowagerie. Toorah was child of Norgwinup's old age— a favorite with her father and with her big grizzly-bear brother, Poke. Inasmuch as Sowagerie had almost crawled on his belly to kiss the soiled hem of Poke's garment, he regarded Toorah, Poke's sister, as a person more wonderful still. The vibrations of her hand in his gave him a thrill long and sweet. He had seen no such girl ever before. She roused in him a sharp sense of his personal unfitness of appearance.

Much as he wanted to meet her again right away, he was somehow impelled to hide whenever she came in sight. He simply wanted to crawl out of himself, and that is the very thing he began to do. He cut the sharp leaves of a yucca bush. Binding them firmly together with a buckskin string, he devised a hair-brush. Laboriously he begun working the tangled knots and twisted snarls out of his faded hair. Stubbornly the gnarled mass yielded to the savage strokes of the crude brush. Sowagerie soon had it all straightened out at the sacrifice of a few fistfuls of hair. He stroked his hand down his head, smiling oddly at the smooth feel of it. He parted it in the middle of his head and, after several frustrating attempts succeeded in braiding it into two neat whips, weaving into them and around them, two strips of bright red rag he had salvaged from somewhere. With these dangles hanging from behind his ears and down across his breast, he regarded himself in a clear pool—what a glorious transformation!

He put a few brave dabs of red and blue paint on his face and looked in the pool again—he was a chief! With ingenuity kindled by the magic touch of soft hands, he got from somewhere a fiery red shirt and a pair of beaded buckskin trousers with fringe along either side. Also, with resourceful resolution, he took from somewhere a pair of new moccasins with artistic designs worked across the toes. More gallant than all else, he obtained a high hat with a wide brim — a hat which had been taken from one of the twelve dead white men dragged down out of the brush.

When he faced himself over the clear water again, he resolved to hide no more from Toorah, but to be on display whenever she came near to him, and to get near her and magnify his wonderful self before her eyes whenever possible.

He was Sowagerie no more. Not only had he crawled out of his old self, like a butterfly out of a caterpillar, but he had taken a new name. A new name seemed indispensable to his new ambition. He was Posey.

Poke and Hatch both had taken their names from two dashing cowboys. Tobuck-ne-ab, the young chief of Allan Canyon, had stolen the name of another cowboy and had become Mancos Jim. Sowagerie had admired the fine outfit and the superfine nerve of a young fellow called Bill Posey, so he followed the lead of greatness and became Posey. Beogah, his brother, appropriated the name of old Dorrity's horse-wrangler, Johnny Scott, and became Scotty.

The remarkable thing about all these self-bestowed names is the way they stuck like printer's ink, completely obliterating the old name within a few months. Even Old Chee, Posey's renegade father, took a new name and became Chee-poots, that is, Old Man Chee.

Gorged with gain and glory from the fight at La Sal, the Paiutes rounded up and loaded up the abundance of their possessions, and all their numbers but one. They returned to exult in the undefiled forests of Elk Mountain. They howled the splendor of their exploits in a more exultant key than ever before, going into wild transports of delight. There they waited again for some one to come after them in battle array. From the beetling rims of the mountain they looked hopefully away to the regions eastward, longing for the sight of men, horses, and outfits to make the long days interesting and profitable. Surely Uncle Sam would not disappoint them this time when they had killed more than four times as many white men as they had killed when they awaited here before.

No one came. The last ripple of the affair at the horse-ranch seemed to blow away with the autumn winds. The tribe scattered in peace to their various old haunts as if nothing unusual had smeared the summer with blood.

Hatch, lusting for more fame, went over among the Uncompahgre Indians to display some of his fine horses and other plunder, but they feared he would get them into trouble, so they turned him over to the law. He was detained for a little while in a chain gang there, but soon came back in peace and safety to San Juan.

No one was ever made to answer for the death of any one of the seventeen white men killed that year by the Paiutes! The taking of life, the destruction of property, the disturbance, the anguish, and the expense it entailed were never brought in any serious charge against these lawless Paiutes, and not one of them was ever made to answer for it. They carried the game

of murder and robbery to a successful and profitable
finish. It was a good game. They liked it! Why should
they not plan more games of the same kind? They
did. They continued to plan them and play them for
forty years.

No member of the tribe reacted with keener relish
to the big drama that year than Sowagerie, now called
Posey. To him the grim drama expressed life, love,
and the royal road to glory. Yet his promotion to man-
hood, as indicated by his reflection in the pool, was
not without its peculiar cost. When he was ragged and
beggarly, Poke had tolerated him as the turncoat's
son—a nuisance too trivial to be noticed. But now,
when the turncoat's son rose up with a great imposing
name, with gorgeous and imposing dress, and with
eager eyes always on the choice little sister, Toorah,
the old grizzly-bear brother turned away in disgust.
"Pu-neeh!" he grunted, with an impatient flip of his
hand.

Pu-neeh is the Paiute word for skunk, and so far
as Poke was concerned, that was Sowagerie's new
name.

The wealth of live stock and treasure gathered by
the Paiutes at the horse-ranch and at La Sal slipped
out of their wasteful hands in an incredibly short
time. Their wild orgies of the big raid were, like a
child's game, soon over. Their return to normalcy was
a return to rags and poverty. Again they stole to keep
body and soul together. The ill-gotten horses and
saddles, and the clothes stripped from the dead, disappeared with the summer leaves or became so bedraggled with improper use and abuse as to be
unrecognizable. But they hung to the fine guns with
persistent instinct. Already the bow and arrow had
come to be more of a symbol than a dependable weapon.

Normalcy found them living again like leeches on the struggling little Mormon settlement. They stole horses, cattle, anything, everything, till the colony's existence became a vexed and bitter problem. Hatch, Sanop, Mike and Tuvagutts set the pace, while the newly- aroused Posey, the two Grasshoppers, and other small fry kept step to the best of their ability.

Navaho Frank and his nephew, young Bitseel, with no farflung raids to distract their attention from business, aspired to excel the whole Paiute tribe in stripping the settlers of everything not under lock and key. Frank was husky and powerful, built of the kind of stuff and in the kind of way to last a hundred years. He laughed loud in contempt at the pleadings of the toilers in Bluff, and at the sage teachings and warnings of their mediator and interpreter, Thales Haskel.

Toorah's imperious brother took no stock in the stale feud between the Chee-poots people and their old neighbors at Navaho Mountain. If the renegades had made lifelong enemies by crowding in where they had no business to go, they had themselves to thank for it. Bitseel was invited and made welcome at the *ducki* game and at other forms of entertainment in the wickiup of Poke, the old grizzly, and Poke returned the visits at the hogan of Bitseel's uncle across the river.

In these visits among the Navahos, and everywhere he went, Poke took Toorah, the little sister, with him, or made one of her three other brothers, Hatch, Bishop or Teegre, responsible for her keeping. The arrangement seemed to be made to forestall Posey's ardent ambitions. The brothers had no objection to her meeting with anyone else. If anything, they seemed to approve of the stalwart young Navaho, Bitseel, to whose home she often went with them.

So *Pu-neeh*, the skunk, alias Posey, alias Sowagerie, had to get into her company by stealth, if at all, and to get out of it by the same difficult and dangerous trail. It was extremely hazardous business. He knew that if the old grizzly, Poke, should find him or his tracks, something terrible would happen.

Poke's aversion for the Paiute renegades who had come back practically naked from their boasted withdrawal to Navaho Mountain, made him doubly dear to Bitseel. Bitseel exulted in the old bear's good fellowship when the Chee people were there to see him enjoy it. He was enjoying what they wanted very much to have, and what would have been their inheritance if they had not been turncoats and had not run away to Navaho Mountain where they made so much sorrow for Bitseel's father, Tsabekiss, and his family.

Bitseel watched eagerly for the Chee family to come to his vicinity. He watched eagerly too for the other renegades to come with them—not that he had a kindly thought for one soul, old or young, among the beggarly ranks, but he wanted to gloat over them. More than that, he had a biting eagerness to come in contract with Posey. He hated every one of them who had been there as troublemakers for his father's kindred, but that hatred had focussed on Posey, who had a way of thrusting forth his tongue in snakelike enmity. Bitseel had discovered Posey's weakness for *ducki* and he resolved to exploit that weakness to a finish.

When he first saw Posey, the gaudy butterfly, in his new finery—red shirt, beaded moccasins, great hat, and gorgeous name—his eyes opened wide as the eyes of a cat spying an unsuspecting sparrow. He watched for a chance to flash the deck before his arrogant hissing enemy. The chance was soon found! Posey had been sharpening his wits all summer for this very moment, playing *ducki* for days at a time on the beetling rims of Elk Mountain, and at other camps where his people had nothing to do but eat and kill time. Posey figured he had his wits honed down to razor edge. The time was ripe for a contest with the insufferable Bitseel, his enemy and rival. It was highly fitting now that he be the conquering chief he had become, that he trim this detested Navaho in the way he had always longed to do.

Posey and Bitseel seated themselves each side of a blanket secluded in the willows where they would not be disturbed, though some of the Navaho's friends stood watching. Posey was confident and defiant, he had evolved from the stupor of his childhood. This was his day of triumph. But Bitseel also had been sharpening his wits —not just all summer, but month in and month out for several years. He had doggedly pursued his goal —mastering the technique of *monte* and *cooncan* always with his renegade adversary in mind.

Here in the williow they began the game with cartridges, working up to small silver, and then to dollars. Posey won from the first, stacking his winnings in a tormenting pile which Bitseel eyed with a distressed expression of disappointment. With every good play Posey let off exultant jibes at his adversary who seemed never to guess that the Paiutes had been playing *ducki* nine tenths of the time while they had been away. But Bitseel played gamely on, cursing his luck under his breath.

Then the tide slowly turned. That tormenting pile of silver went over to the other side of the blanket.

Posey frowned, found less and less to say, and went on, of course, with the game. He was sure that his superior wits would prevail, and that his remaining three dollars would suffice to turn the tide. The three dollars wasted away, coin at a time, and went to build up the tantalizing pyramid of his daring enemy.

Posey found himself sitting there, broke and humiliated, right in the middle of this supreme game to which he had been looking forward for months. It was more than a game; it was a battle. So much hung on the way it turned. He must by all means win back part of the money with which he began —that much to save his honor. Yes, and he must by all means do more. He must cut some eye-teeth for this devilish Navaho as he had prepared and resolved to do.

Desperate as he contemplated the situation, he loosed his beaded moccasins from his feet, demanded that they be matched by their full value, and staked them on a bet. And —curses! He lacked an ace of spades. Bitseel had it, and he added the princely foot-gear to his pile. Now Posey must not let a muscle of his hand or of his face betray the sting this gave him — he was a chivalrous chief —his luck would change.

He staked the proud hat under which he came riding from the glory at La Sal. The avaricious Navaho won it — took it without a word of exultation, and instead of adding it to the pile as a future pawn in the game, handed it over right there to another Navaho in payment of an account.

That was almost more than the Paiute's proud soul could bear in silence— the hat had gone beyond recall! Still he resolved to keep his anguish well concealed. Any show of pain would delight his enemy and prove his defeat. He would sit right there and prove his superior stuff if it took all night! He peeled off his beautiful red shirt; Bitseel took it over without moving a muscle of his face.

No robot of bronze could have performed with fewer words or less motion than that son of old Tsa-bekiss as he waged his battle through victory after victory. Posey's taunting jibes echoed away to mocking silence. The fight went on as between two automatons wound up to run for a given length of time in a set pattern.

Ducki becomes a mysterious anesthetic: deadening its victim to the blows he receives in the latter part of the game and at the same time inflaming him with a wild passion to win at all hazards. Dazed and half naked, Posey saw the red shirt slip from his hands. He retained just enough concern for the world around him to be sure that none of his people were near enough to see. Nothing stirred in the jungle of willows where they had found shade and seclusion, and approaching evening offered no cause for un-easiness.

He still had the dashing, fringed trousers, with glittering bead-work along the seams. From his naked waist to his bare feet, these elegant trousers repre-sented his only remaining claim to the glory of his new-found self. He considered them desperately. What if they should go? D---the difference! He would rather take a chance on humiliating this infernal thief than own the most kingly breeches ever worn by a chief.

He removed the fringed beauties from his legs and folded them neatly with trembling hands. Hope, hate, and direst curses boiled through his fevered mind. He was devoting them with awful heart-burnings to a final shot in this exasperating battle where he

could resort to neither words nor weapons. Surely
fortune would have to turn in his favor — he had
never known it to go so steadily in the wrong direction
before.

With nervous fingers and twitching lips he manipulated his cards as he sat there in his breech-cloth,
studying Bitseel's metallic face. The beaded trousers
slipped away on a jack of hearts! Nonchalantly the
Navaho added them to his tantalizing pile of kingly
apparel by the saucy little pyramid of silver. Surely
the devil was in the *ducki!*

Bitseel contemplated his enemy's nakedness, and
the bronze muscles of his face relaxed. *"Hacoon!"*
(Come on!) he bantered, looking to see if there might
be a ring, a bracelet, or anything else on the Paiute's
perspiring body which would be worth playing for.
Posey's black eyes flashed. Bitseel's friends betrayed
their amusement as they looked on. One of them re-
marked that Posey should be quite happy now—nothing
at all about which to worry. Another of them wore the
proud hat with which Posey had come boastingly into
the game.

Mortified, and angry, and hopeless, the naked
Paiute rose to his feet and looked for a way to keep
out of sight till darkness would shelter him on his
way to some kind of covering. He looked back at the
little group sitting in merriment still around the
blanket. There was nothing to do — he didn't so much
as run out his tongue at his enemy as he looked for
the darkest place among the willows.

The little sister, Toorah, must not see him now.
She must never know a thing about it. Yet Bitseel
might wear these things for her benefit! Before she
could have time to see these heroic clothes on some other

man, Posey must display himself in a more dashing garb and be prepared with a brave story explaining it all away, and at the same time making himself more a hero than before.

Resolute as if his very life were staked on this issue, Posey nailed the very first unguarded horse left on the hills by the people of the fort. Then with his fair ability as a trader and his unfair ability as a thief, he lost no time in replacing his butterfly-wings and displaying himself where the dear Toorah could not fail to see him.

CHAPTER SEVEN

SOLDIER CROSSING

The cool air and the green grass of the upper country lured the Paiutes away from the heated sandhills and cliffs around Bluff during much of the summertime. At the foot of the Blue Mountain two big cattle companies put on a fine show every day—fat cattle, riproaring horses, bronco-busting cowpunchers with guns on both hips. These latter were ever ready to enter a sociable fight to the death with but half an invitation.

Indolent or not, the Paiutes had always a perfect mania for quick action. If the world seemed to lag, they made it their business to prod it into action. Moreover, three years had passed since the big days at Paiute Spring and La Sal. Something in their Paiute blood begun to murmur at the long monotony.

At South Montezuma, near the foot of Blue Mountain, the Paiutes moved in rather formidable numbers into close proximity to one of the big cow-camps. There they took stock of the prospects for some excitement. It soon transpired that the Indians had in their possession a certain horse. A heated controversy arose between the white men and the people of the wickiups. The cowboys claimed that horse.

As threats flew and tempers flared an Indian named Brooks was shot through the neck. The fight was on! A rousing racket of splendid promise had been set in motion with mighty little effort.

After a rapid succession of signs spelling serious trouble, the cowpunchers decided to look for a less

dangerous place to stay than their camp on South
Montezuma. They hurried their horses into the corral
to make a prompt departure. While they roped the
animals to work or to ride, a storm of bullets came
whistling around them, peppering the poles of the log
fence within disturbing proximity.

In panicky haste the cowhands hitched four big
mules to a wagon loaded high with bedding and provisions. Then the mounted men with their herd of
saddles-horses surrounded it — as a kind of body-
guard while it started up the hill under the lash. In
this way they hoped to get the conspicuous, slow-
moving wagon safely out of the danger-zone.

When the Indians saw that the white men intended
to take the wagon up Devil-Canyon road, they quit
firing and seemed to give up the fight. The rumbling
big wagon, yanked along by the fiery mules, and
surrounded by the roar of steel-shod hoofs, progressed up the hill in peace. As the cowmen rode out into the
sagebrush prairie to the south everything looked rosy.
They breathed a sigh of deep relief as men who had
walked the rim of a rumbling volcano.

Two miles out on that road to the southwest they
approached Roundup Ground, a little valley between
low hills mottled with groves of oak. When the wagon
and its roughriders reached the center of this friendly-
looking glen, pandemonium broke loose. Rifle shots
thundered from all around. One of the big wheeler-
mules fell kicking in his harness. The lead mules jerked
sharply around as if they wanted to climb into the
wagon for safety.

The teamster sprang to the ground in confusion
and tried to catch one of the loose horses. Dolf Lusk
was wounded in the hip—another cowboy in the foot.

The other men stumbled up from their dead horses and tried desperately to catch something else to ride. Cowboys bolted headlong in every direction — anywhere to dodge death as it shrieked after them from those groves of oak.

The Indians shot down the last frantic mule thrashing around the wagon. Triumphantly they rode out from their cover to gather the booty. They rounded up that string of valuable horses, stripped the wagon of its load, and the big mules of such straps in the harness as they happened to fancy.

As a farewell token of their cordial regards, they heaped dry limbs over the wagon and set it afire. The old irons of that wagon were scattered in Roundup Ground for years after. Leaving the wagon in a red blaze over the tangle of dead mules, the Paiutes moved deliberately away with their plunder and their rejoicing progeny. Ahead of them was the Big Trail with its maze of ledges and rims from which no Paiute fugitive had ever been dragged back. They decided now to head for that trail. They would lead the *Mericats* (Americans) far into its mazes before turning them back or offering them to the crows and coyotes. They would not be in such a hurry that the Mericats could not tell which way they had gone. And surely they would be coming right away in hot pursuit —how delightful!

The Paiutes figured that when the big game was on they should have their wives and children right along with them. This was not only to forestall these weaker ones from getting the worst of the deal if they were found alone. It was also to enable them to enjoy their full share of these thrilling contests. In addition, the fathers wanted their children to breathe the inspiring atmosphere of the most delightful occasions to keep in full vigor the old fighting spirit of the tribe.

So the Paiutes took their people old and young into every promising situation. They took their goats, all their camp rag-shag, and by all means their indispensable, mangy dogs. Their domestic life—if any part of such a life could be called domestic—was preserved more vigorously in war than in peace. When they moved from that burning wagon up into the tall timber, it was a great jubilating family reunion — aunts, uncles, nieces, nephews, and every tottering *nanipoots* (old man) still clinging to the frail fabric of life.

The gaudy Posey, with his two whips of ebony hair and all his bright plumage, was prominent whereever prominence was possible without being hazardous. He rode a good horse and carried a good rifle. To his way of thinking he was indispensable to the fighting machinery of the tribe. He couldn't ride often in Poke's august shadow, yet he could parade his imposing figure now and then before Toorah's appreciative eyes. She rewarded his efforts with a grunt or by coyly hiding her face.

The old grizzly-bear, Poke, austere and uncompromising, with his villainous, inky mustache vertical across his mouth, looked at the Navaho-Mountain upstart with cool contempt. This Sowagerie, masquerading under the white man's name of Posey—he was *Pu-neeh!* Nothing more, nothing less.

Posey knew that Poke's displeasure was not to be underestimated as a source of possible danger. Still he was impelled to get near the little sister as often as possible. The stress of the new game of waiting for the Mericats made it possible for him to see her at frequent intervals. To further add to his good luck, his hated Navaho rival was nowhere near and could not see her at all.

On the fifth afternoon the scouts of the camp reported Mericats in sight. Cowboys and soldiers. A big company! They seemed to be *too itch tobuck* (heap mad). What a lively promise for the game to be played! The angrier the better! Just so the Mericats could not sneak up alongside!

Up Hammond Canyon and across Elk Mountain the jubilating Paiute family strung out in a long procession, pretending to be running in fear. They kept tantalizingly out of rifle-range with exultant chuckles. Every so often they made it a point to stimulate the wrath of the Mericats by leaving some extra fine cow-horse behind with their ferocious regards written on him in fresh red lines of blood and old scabs from ears to hoofs showing cruel abuse with whips, spurs, and saddles.

The Indians chose their course with murderous precision, all the while feigning to be in heedless flight from their pursuers. To the Paiutes the wild country was as familiar as an old book. To the posse it was undecipherable. On past a dozen rock-ribbed elbows the Paiutes ran, in any of which they could have wiped out their pursuers or hurled them back in confusion. But why should they stop the fun so soon? Its progress, mile after mile, involved them in no danger. Every one of them, from the tottering old *nanipoots* down to the smallest toddling papoose was gloating and snickering for every rod they covered.

From Wooden Shoe Buttes on the western slope of the mountain, the schemers turned southwest down among a maze of precipitous rims. The posse stormed

along after them, just out of rifle-range, unaware
of trap after trap through which they were being led.
One thing, and one only induced the posse to slacken
their pace a bit—that was a gentle hint in the shape
of a few bullets plowing up the dust too close to mis-
understand.

The Mericats held to the red man's tracks, up and
down, left and right, over sand and hillside and rocks.
They followed stupidly into a deep box canyon where
they could have been shut up like rats in a trap, but
Poke and his people rode on dove-like from this advantage as they had from others. On and on the Paiutes
went, holding to their familiar trail towards the north
rim of Mossback Mesa.

When the cowboys and soldiers got out of the box
of White Canyon, they saw the Indians climbing the
mountain to the south. Exasperated to a frenzy with
this tantalizing business, they made for that mountain
on the lope. How strange that it never dawned on them
that they were at the mercy of the Indians and had been
for days past.

The Paiutes had resolved to go the full length of
the Old Trail—to renew acquaintance with the exploits of their fathers—but they planned to hurl back
the foolish posse from this point in the White Canyon.
Accordingly they stopped on an upper shelf of the
mountain and peeped from behind big rocks along
the rim. This time, when the white men came too near
they shot the two lead men instead of the dusty trail.
The posse dropped quickly back to the first possible
cover taking refuge in a little gulch. They had to hug
the underside of a ledge to keep out of sight. There
they were pinned for the rest of the day with no retreat. If any horse moved enough to expose his head

or tail to the sharp-shooters on the ledge above, he was shot through.

From their natural fortress on the upper ledge the brown warlords called mockingly to the Mericats "Come on up!" But the Mericats, sweating 'neath the ledge in a huddle in the July heat, heard their wounded comrades calling for water and dared not so much as peep from their cover. The day became long and terrible. Night held no assurance that the Paiutes would not come stealthily down and rake their shelter with bullets from the side. Why the lawless band did not do that very thing, and leave no one to live to tell the tale, must be credited to some persistent element of human kindness.

One of the wounded men was a soldier named Worthington. The other was a cowboy named Wilson, but going by the nickname of Rowdy. Pleadingly they called for water. Under the direct rays of the scorching July sun their voices grew weaker and weaker as the afternoon wore on. They could still be heard calling faintly when the sun sank behind the irregular horizon.

Darkness released the posse from their crowded prison under that rocky rim, but they did not go with water to their dying comrades. Instead they hurried away for their lives hunting water for themselves in White Canyon through which they had pursued their seeming prey with such dare-devil eagerness the day before. Now they were taking all that the Paiutes had generously allowed them. So were the two wounded men. They lay helpless on the hillside while the whole gloating tribe came down and incited their wolf-like dogs to torment the two captives to death.

Oh, who was Uncle Sam? Who were the fighting men in blue coats with brass buttons? Who were those cowboys with their trusty guns and loud bluster? They had cowered all day under a little rim ledge like whipped dogs. They had been glad to sneak away in the darkness without so much as a word to their wounded comrades. They had gone back the way they came—they hadn't ever fired one promising shot!

With eager skill, the savages stripped the soldier of his uniform with the bright buttons, and the cowboy of his fancy boots and shirt and other things. This last was divided among the lions of the tribe. One of them received a silver watch which was found later by Joshua Stevens where the Big Trail leads up the sandslide out of North Gulch. Another of them got the blue coat for which he was known ever after as Soldier-Coat.

That night, on the high rim of Mossback Mesa, the staccato chant of their war-song echoed away into the wild solitudes which they loved. These solitudes had been the security of their fathers for unwritten ages past. Each of the charted death-traps through which they had led their prey had a cherished legend handed down from the past. Now this latest death trap had been glorified by the two mangled forms lying at the foot of the hills below. Similar places waited on the trail ahead—places known and loved of old for their sure defense of the fighting fathers.

It would have been a huge delight and perfectly safe pastime for Poke and his people to have worried that demoralized bunch of soldiers and cowpunchers all the way back to South Montezuma. But the Paiutes had a plan for something of greater significance to them. They had resolved to go on over the Old Trail. They would revel the length of its legendary course and drink again of its glory and celebrated history.

This trail was new to Posey, yet it was to him as water to a young duck. Though his father had been

one of those offensive secessionists from the main
tribe, still the deep tribal instinct had not changed in
the least. If the Old Trail lacked any essential of
coming to him as his long-lost self, then the little
sister more than compensated to him for that lack.
When Posey saw Toorah's face in the bewitching
glimmer of the camp-fire, or when he caught sight
of her on her pony—her skirt a dazzle of bright colors—
he envisioned the Old Trail as the perfect dreamland
from South Montezuma to the Pagahrit. Always the
brightest angel of that dreamland was Poke's little
sister.

From Mossback Mesa the Old Trail led across the
cliffbound tributaries of Red Canyon, skirted the
dizzy rim of the yawning Colorado River, and entered
the deeply-cut ravines of North Gulch. From these lux-
uriant jungles of black willow, the Indians climbed the
monstrous sand-slide and entered the loneliest wilderness ever created—the region of the remote and
mysterious Pagahrit where heat-legions resolve themselves into strange and misleading figures of mirage,
and where lost echoes become disturbing voices from
another world.

Here in this enchanted region of the Pagahrit,
walled off on three sides by the deep chasms of the
San Juan and Colorado Rivers and on the other side by
yawning canyons and high rims, the Paiutes proceeded
to hold a high and holy carnival as the place and
occasion demanded. The people of Bluff had hidden
many of their cattle for safekeeping in this far-away
corner. With these, the jubilant tribe made lavish
offerings to their gods of war. They gormandized on
the finest young animals and stuffed their mangy dogs
to a state of nausea. They killed cattle wantonly to sat-
isfy their blood-lust inherited from bloody ancestors.

They killed cattle with their guns, but to preserve the supreme art of their fathers, they also shot them with arrows, indifferent to all which they killed or wounded. Cows fled distractedly over the hills with long arrows bristling from their sides. Before these wild men left the country, every breeze was stifling with the scent of rotting carcasses.

For seven days the Paiutes celebrated near the abrupt shores of the lake, rehearsing the ancient legend of the man-eating monster hiding deep in its mazes of sea-weed. Old men of the tribe told of similar celebrations here in the distant past when Navahos or Shoshones lay dead and mangled on the trail behind. They chanted it in concert and danced at close formation around their fires. The fierce rhythm of their songs drifted away over the lake to return in ghostly echoes from the bare cliff beyond.

A tottering *nanipoots* piloted them away from the lake, for the old pathway led over solid rock where no betraying track would be left behind. But this was not for the purpose of foiling any chance pursuer— they had no hopes of being pursued—it was simply an indispensable feature of the old program—the kind of precautions which robbers learn by instinct to preserve. For this same reason they forded the San Juan in a region where their tracks would be quickly obliterated. At various places they made devious turns and detours inexplicable to anyone outside of the tribe. From the end of the trail south of the river, they sought the shady places of Navaho Mountain to rest and sleep —and to play long and delightful games of *ducki* before they returned to the big herds and looked for new prospects of excitement.

CHAPTER EIGHT

OLD GRIZZLY

Now back again in his native mountain, Posey courted a little publicity by thrusting himself forward as guide. He knew the country in detail. He could tell where all the important things had happened. Off there to the southeast he had helped to follow the tracks of two trespassing white men and had made a rich haul. He wanted especially to tell all this and his part therein where Toorah could hear.

Of late, however, he had had to be sharply on the alert for the appearance of the wide black hat and that straight-up-and-down mustache, lest her brother, the big grizzly, should drop his ponderous paw on what he regarded as a poor little skunk. Of late the old bear had given Posey a terrible chill—he hardly dared to look at the little sister any more, even when the coast seemed clear.

The occasion of this chill developed from events on the Big Trail. The Paiutes lived together in peace only when they were united tooth and nail against their enemies. After the fight they busied themselves quarreling and fighting with each other over the plunder. When they rounded up that herd of saddle-horses in the little valley near South Montezuma where the big mules lay dead, a slashing pacer dashed over the hills. The Indians following him gave up, not daring to venture so far alone lest they run into an ambush. But Buck Grasshopper had set his heart on that particular pinto pacer. Racing on alone, he brought the coveted animal back. The next morning when each man picked his horse for the day, Poke came first among the lions for his share, and threw his rope on the pinto.

"That's my horse," protested Grasshopper. "I brought him back when everybody else had quit."

"Shut up!" growled the old grizzly, not deigning so much as to give the boy a look. On the remainder of the trip all the big chiefs recognized Poke's first right to the pinto pacer.

Grasshopper watched the splendid animal skip bird-like over the hills with his load. Although he half agreed with the tribal law that might is right, he longed to ride that horse just once to get the bird-like thrill.

In the delay of crossing the San Juan some of the horses strayed away over the bald rocks. The pacer was among them. Hunters went looking for tracks in three directions, but Buck Grasshopper found their trail and followed up a canyon and off over a mesa before he overtook the runaway horses. Alone and far from the outfit he took this as his opportunity to try the pinto pacer. He would ride him but a little way as he took the horses back the way they came.

Meanwhile the other hunters found where Buck had taken the tracks. Since that was about the direction the camp wanted to go, the whole tribe headed off up the canyon where Grasshopper had gone. The old grizzly bear was in the lead. At a sharp turn around the point they met the lost horses with Grasshopper behind them on the pacer.

Poke raised his head and stared from under his wide hat, while his lip became visible below the walrus-tusk mustache. The whole long string of Indians, squaws, papooses, *nanipoots*, and all slowed down to a stand-still behind him. No one dared to insult his dignity of leadership by passing on ahead.

Dashing madly to the offending youth, Poke snatched him from the pony and leaped with him to the ground. *"Avahte!"* (Dog!) he foamed. Around his waist the old grizzly, Poke, carried a rawhide hog-string. Loosing this with furious fingers he doubled it up as a heavy whip and beat the struggling Buck with all his might. Most of the blows fell on the boy's shoulders and arms, but some of them reached his head and cut like a knife into his face.

Posey, who had been riding with as much adjacency to the grizzly chief as his courage permitted, drew up in terrified surprise at the suddenness and fury of the whole affair. He saw the hard lash leave its red welt on Buck's flesh. He saw the loop-end of it sink into Buck's cheek. With a shudder he contemplated what would happen to him if he were found unduly near to the little sister.

All the same, when fear measures strength with love, unusual things may happen, for "love casteth out all fear." After their first day of rest at the mountain, Poke went hunting in the tall timber. Posey had to go that morning on the track of a run-away horse. Returning late in the afternoon he found the coast clear of anyone to challenge his presence wherever he wanted to go among the wickiups. It was a camp of squaws and papooses—no one to mock at his thrilling stories.

At the headquarters of the old bear he caught sight of Toorah with two older women, weaving a basket. Venturing nearer he looked into their bower of carefully-placed limbs. Leaning himself against a little post at the side of the doorway, he told the women he had just made a long ride and was hungry as a coyote. They invited him to some venison roasting on the coals. Seating himself on the ground by the fire, he cut off a chunk of the juicy meat and began to eat. While he ate he began telling of his childhood days here at Navaho Mountain, of the big grass and fat game while the Navahos languished in prison.

He found unusual freedom to relate thrilling adventures he had not thought of for a long time— some, in fact, about which he had never heard before. Toorah's pretty fingers went on with her weaving but he knew she listened even though she seldom looked up. He told about hunting deer and bighorn in the deep timber, of riding wild colts with nothing but a rawhide thong on their chins, of following Mike over among the monuments on the track of two white men with valuable outfits.

The little sister liked it. He knew she liked it. She cast sly glances at him and he grew mighty as he related the daring part he took. From furtive sidelongs at her he contemplated his own dashing figure: the gallant hat, the ebony whips interwoven with flashing red, the beaded footgear, the fringed trousers. He throught of the brave dabs of paint on his face, his irresistable good looks and kingly appearance. He contemplated Toorah, plump and coy and beautiful. He scanned her bewitching skirt of red and yellow and blue —she was infinitely more powerful than her bearish brother, yet she was not bearish at all.

Posey sat with his face away from the entrance, intent on his story and the magic reaction it was getting as it progressed. He took no note of time. When the older women showed their lack of interest, he addressed himself directly to the little sister. She raised her eyes more often now, and even grunted her relish for the pictures of his heroism.

"I outran Bitseel as he followed their track," he boasted. "I passed him and his father."

"*Oaakerum!*" (Yes!) she cooed in pleasant admiration.

"I was right next to Mike when he ---"

She sprang from the blanket on which she sat and gripped his hand excitedly. "They are coming! My brother is coming!" she urged in a hoarse whisper, pulling him towards the doorway.

His fingers closed around her soft hand and he yielded readily to her persuasion. It was the charming touch of the hand he had gripped in the thicket of birch willows at La Sal.

She drew him quickly through the doorway. "*Tooish apane!*" (Hurry up!) she breathed in fear of being heard, at the same time returning the fervor of his grip. "Come some other time. I'll watch for you."

He had but turned his head reluctantly to look for the nearest cover when a shadow fell over them both —the shadow of a great wide hat. They looked up at the unforbearing up-and-down mustache and two fierce eyes drawn down to narrow slits. "*Pu-neeh!* Renegade pup!" spat the grizzly big brother, his long fingers fumbling at the knot of his rawhide hogstring. The girl seized her brother's hand, her eyes pleading in terror. In trying to throw her off Poke made as if he would strike her.

Quick as a cat and with strength and daring to his own surprise, Posey snatched a heavy stick from the ground. "Don't you dare to strike her!" he hissed, raising the club in defiance.

Yielding from habit to the little sister, and yielding to the skunk for his firmness in her defense, Poke gave up his effort to loose the knot in the hogstring. But he glared at the renegade's son with unyielding aversion. "Turncoat! Skunk!" he grunted, fierce fire leaping in his narrow eyes. "Get out of here! Never dare to speak to my sister again." He motioned with his long fingers for Posey to be gone at once. "Remember—Never again!"

The skunk caught a glimpse of the girl's assuring smile as he turned towards his father's wickiup.

Ten days more at Navaho Mountain and that glutted snarl of Paiutes would have been clawing at each other's throats. Sanop and his boys sided with Buck Grasshopper. Soldier-Coat and Mancos Jim held aloof from the quarrel, while Mike and Tuvagutts nursed grievances of their own. Chee-poots wanted his sons, Posey and Scotty, to retire with him to the tall timber, and let the others go with their quarrels back to their own country. None of that for Posey! The stigma of desertion was already the shame of his life. He didn't want to see the tall timber unless Toorah was there.

Poke and his brothers, loaded with their share of the plunder, their lion's share, went down to visit old Tsabekiss, the Big Navaho. Toorah and the rest of Norgwinup's posterity dared do nothing but follow him. Those not of that posterity, unless they were invited to go, dared do nothing but remain behind.

The big gang broke up into a dozen factions. They easily might have been separated for a long time but for the steady lure of ready plunder at the Bluff fort, and at the big herds around Blue Mountain. Back to the little Mormon settlement each clan straggled in its own due time. Every family and every individual among them vehemently denied having taken any

part in the fight at South Montezuma or at Soldier
Crossing, as the place of the killing in white canyon
has been known ever since.

The Paiutes were not much richer but carried mute
evidence here and there of their involvement in the
carnage. But if ever Uncle Sam or anyone else ever
entertained a notion of making any kind of reprisals
for the robberies and murders, no hint of it was ever
whispered to anyone of the tribe. From their point
of view they had proved again that robbery and murder
is safe and interesting business, and that Uncle Sam
was unable or disinclined to make serious objection.
The idea of their ever being punished became a joke
in their camps. They still had peace and freedom to
go where they wanted to go, and to do just about as they
pleased. There was nothing to hinder them from
staging more and better parties, if ever they could
unite to make the start.

But in that problem of uniting, they seemed to be
meeting a growing difficulty—Mike and his renegades
returning like prodigals to the fold, brought to the tribe
certain persistent elements of discord which grew like
"leaven in three measures of meal which threatened
to leaven the whole lump." It seemed that the only
way for them to unite at all was in some rousing out-
burst against the common enemy, the white invaders.
As soon as that trouble blew over, the union dissolved.

CHAPTER NINE

WHITE MEDICINE MAN

Poverty is a state of mind. A disease! With the Paiutes it was chronic—the heritage of untold generations past. All the gains of their latest raid melted away while they stayed in hiding. When they began again to depend on the beef and horses of the little Mormon settlement, they cut sharply into the thriving business of Bitseel and his kinsman, Navaho Frank.

Hatch and Mike and Tuvagutts took up the business in a kind of wholesale way, setting up a sort of chain of receivers and deliverers which threatened to suck the country dry of every animal not kept under guard. The two Grasshoppers and Bob and Posey toiled aspiringly after these greater minds. Sanop and his two boys specialized in robbing the settlers of everything and anything they could carry away.

Six weeks after Poke left Navaho Mountain to visit old Tsabekiss, the Chee-poots people found him camped near Bluff, but Toorah was not with him. She was not in any of the wickiups of the Norgwinup family. They refused to talk to Posey, and he and Scotty hunted for her in vain. Had Poke left her with Tsabekiss? Had they sold her to the Navahos to become the property of Bitseel? Posey knew of a Paiute girl who had been traded to the Navahos for ten head of horses. It looked quite possible that the old grizzly, in his wrath, might have taken that means of keeping his sister from the despised skunk. To Posey the thought was extremely disturbing.

Aside from this strange and alarming disappearance of the little sister, conditions reverted with the Paiutes to much the same as they had been before the glory procession over the Old Trail. They played *ducki* and more *ducki*. Every day, in every wickiup and in most of the Navaho hogans, they had a game of *ducki*, cooncan, monte, or some similar racket for gain without cost. Sitting on a blanket in the shade, or by the fire if the weather were cold, and gaining or losing values without sweat or exertion—that was the life of greatness for the Paiutes. And every one of them thought himself great.

If they could find no Navaho or Mexican to skin on the *ducki* blanket, they skinned each other. Whenever they were not busy prowling the range, or eating, or sleeping, or begging, they were sure to be enthralled with their gains, or cursing their losses in *ducki*.

If bad medicine followed the flip of the cards for too long at a time, and the range were too closely guarded for livestock stealing, they had to subsist on the meager earnings of their squaws who bent over the old-time washboards for the Mormons, or scrubbed old pine floors, or hoed weeds, or chopped tough cottonwood limbs into stovewood length.

From their latest raid the Paiutes came to the area of the little colony on the San Juan River like a swarm of locusts, devouring everything before them. In despair the white people appealed to Haskel to stay the rapacity of the camps on every side. Eager to do everything he could for the well-being of the colony he had been sent to help protect, the old gray-beard went patiently from lodge to lodge, visiting the leading thieves of both tribes. Stooping, and old and slow with measured step he entered silently to sit in the smelly wickiups or hogans, and look at the wondering inmates till they became eager to know his business.

"*Impo ashanty?*" (What do you want?) they asked from all sides of the sagebrush fire. But Haskel looked studiously down his nose, fixing his gaze on the coals while their susceptibilities worked into a keen pitch. They saw dignity and disappointment in his sage bearing. His presence stirred guilty memories. What would he say now? Most of them had mocked his message before, but every one had been impressed then as now with his forceful personality.

They knew he would never speak till they gave him urgent invitation by perfect silence. He sat cross-legged on the ground, his head bowed forward. He was a stoic—a heap big chief! They listened, all eyes fixed on his still figure. "*Impo ashanty?*" (What do you want?) pleaded young Henry.

"*Shin-op* (God or the Great Spirit) sent His servants to talk to us." Then the Indians remembered having seen three men come from the north and go after three days in their buckboard up the river. "Shin-op," Haskel continued, after pausing for his words to soak in, "wants us to stay here and be your friends. He tells us that if you go on stealing our horses and cattle, you'll die." The words came with impressive firmness. A hush reigned in the wickiup.

"Maybe you'll get sick and die," he continued slowly, speaking or grunting the words with all the guttural inflection of a native Paiute. "Maybe you will kill each other. Maybe *Shin-op* will send the lightning to strike you. Maybe He will reach out with His unseen hand and touch you and you will wither up like the grass under the burning sun."

He turned his black eyes searchingly from face to face while the silence became oppressive. "If you steal our horses or kill our cattle, you'll die!" he repeated with emphasis.

"Strong medicine!" commented Old Baldy, reverently.

"Good medicine!" added his son, Henry.

"Yes, I'm scared to death of it," sneered Hatch, with mocking gesture.

"Yes, me," grunted Sanop in contempt. "Now I won't dare to look at a Mormon horse nor touch any of their beef even if I'm starving to death."

Posey heard in Haskel's words something unusual, to say the least. He noticed that Poke had respect for them in spite of what Poke's older brother, Hatch, had said.

But Posey's concern, his deep concern, was all for the little sister— What in the world had become of her? Could it be that in the old bear's good will for Tsabekiss he had sold her to him? Would she belong to Bitseel? If he could find some way to win Poke's favor, he would know all about it. Possibly if old Haskel really had the power he pretended to have, he might be induced to bring Toorah back, or to tell where she could be found.

Posey went at first chance, to Haskel's cabin and told the old sage all about it. The old man listened without moving a muscle or looking up. Would Haskel make her brother bring her back? No! Would he find out from the Paiutes where she was? No. Would he for a tip top horse make the kind of medicine that would bring her back? No. Not for a whole band of tip top horses. It was discouraging.

"Listen," pursued Haskel, turning his penetrating eyes straight at Posey when he was about to leave with disgust. "You quit stealing, quit lying, quit wanting to kill some man and get away with his outfit, and *Shin-op* will love you. When *Shin-op* loves you, all your troubles will come out right."

What a poor answer! It sounded like an old squaw. Posey went away in bad humor. Yet brooding still about Toorah, and thinking of her every hour of every day and many a night, he got to thinking more favorably about what Haskel had said. After all, that looked more like a gleam of hope than anything he had found.

Months passed. Nothing happened one way or the other to prove the old medicine man's words. Three times Posey had refrained from taking unguarded horses. Not that he had repented—not Posey. But he wanted to try the virtue of the only medicine he had found. Surely there was something most unusual about Haskel. He was the only one even to hint that the trouble would ever pass away.

Posey rode all the way to the hogan of old Tsabekiss near Navaho Mountain pretending to be on other business, but hoping against hope to find some trace of the little sister. She was not there. After snooping and spying under one pretense or another into a dozen lodges, he felt sure that she had not stayed in that part of the country. Then he prowled around Bitseel's quarters across the river from Bluff, eavesdropping, and watching from cover for long hours at a time. It was all to no purpose.

He went to the Ute reservation in Colorado and nosed through every camp from Merriano Springs to Pine River. He met Utes who knew all of old Norgwinup's family, but either they wouldn't or they couldn't tell him a thing about the old man's baby daughter.

Could it be possible that old grizzly had killed her?

Though Posey could see nothing to indicate that Toorah had ever stayed for long at a time at Bitseel's hogan, nor had been there except in company with her brothers, still Bitseel seemed to know a lot more about Poke and Poke's sentiments than could be accounted for. Possibly he knew all about the little sister —he who could keep silent and preserve a face like a bronze image no matter what tempest of fact or feeling might be surging in his mind.

Once when Posey watched a game of *ducki* back of the old log store in Bluff, he laid a dollar against somebody's bet and won. Then somebody on the other side of the blanket laid five dollars on a certain card, hissing, "Skunk bait!" Posey saw Bitseel looking with his eyes full of contempt and enmity, waiting for him to cover the bet.

Startled and stung, but having just won a dollar, Posey fished his little wad of four dollars from his pocket and covered the bait. It had a fifty-fifty chance of becoming sufficient answer to its own insult. But there was in it something strangely evil—bad medicine, for the very next flip of the cards gave the ten dollars to Bitseel.

"*Ay law! Pu-neeh shi-nizen!*" (Well I declare, I do like skunk meat!) he gloated as he took up the money.

Posey thrust his hands into his empty pockets and stared with bitterness and wonder. Surely that fellow knew things which Posey wanted desperately to know. "Where did you learn to say that?" he half demanded, half pled.

"*Nine kotch pe soogh away*," (I don't know), Bit-seel answered in perfect Paiute with mock innocence. He looked more mysterious still as he assumed that expressionless face beneath that little hat strapped down over his heavy hair with a bridle throat-latch.

While Posey was brooding over Toorah's mysterious disappearance, strange things began happening among the Indians.

Tuvagutts had his camp in a little canyon eight miles east of Bluff. He had selected that as best and safest place from which to spy and strip the range near town. From there he could gather the Mormon's top horses on short notice, take them on to McCracken Mesa and then, by easy stages, to his confederates in the two reservations.

One day in August he rode around, according to his deceitful custom, and entered Bluff from the west so that no one might guess the direction of his camp to which he intended to return after dark. His visit was for the purpose of spying, but incidentally, and to further conceal his purpose, get a load of melons. In the evening he left town bulging with sacks on each side of his saddle, just as a fussy little storm began blowing up from the southwest. In half an hour that little storm had evolved its fussy stage into the majesty of a black storm. Thunder crashed. Sharp splits of lightning reached in fury out of the blackness above.

At what was called the Jump, east of Bluff, four Navahos were about to overtake the old man with his awkward load of melons. A blinding crash shot out from angry clouds, knocking the rider and his horse from the trail as a chipmunk might be blown from a limb with a shot gun. Tuvagutts and his pony lay scrambled in a red blotch. The melons had splattered into nothingness like so much clear water.

News of this tragedy traveled under the lash from camp to camp—Haskel's strange medicine! The report gave Posey a great start. The medicine seemed to be working. Haskel had said maybe lightning would strike them. Thieving old Tuvagutts was one of the very first to come under Haskel's curse. Maybe Posey's troubles would still come out right, if he would abide the conditions.

Then another report raced on the heels of the first: Some mysterious calamity had suddenly overtaken Navaho Frank. Hearty and robust he had lain down on his blanket at night. In the morning his great lungs seemed to have caved in. He had no capacity for breath. He could move, but slowly, with labored step. Working his way at once to Haskel, he begged to live, and promised never to steal another Mormon horse, if Haskel would but intervene for his life.

Some of the people of the northern tribe crossed the river to Frank's hogan, and found him helpless as from an unseen hand. An unseen hand— Haskel had spoken of that unseen hand reaching out to punish them. They worried about it. Bob, the rising young thief, could not get it out of his mind. When he had lain awake four nights dwelling on it with increasing anxiety, he developed a terrible fever, became hysterical and died. It surely looked like deadly medicine, yet Grasshopper and his brother laughed at it.

In his determined search for Toorah, Posey had spied on every camp along up the river into New Mexico. Sometime ago Toorah's brothers, Hatch and Sanop, had gone on a long trip. Maybe Toorah had been taken with them on the unusual, far-away journey. She might even be dead. If any man knew a thing about her, he feared grizzly old Poke too much to breathe a syllable of it to Posey.

Then a strange thing happened! The Chee-poots people had been camping for three weeks at the foot of a high cliff in Cottonwood where big trees sheltered their wickiups. A trail led up to the high bench on the west side of the canyon, but no trail up the east side nearer than a mile away.

Over the brow of that cliff, towering high above them on the east, the desert winds moaned and sighed, sounding at times like a human voice. Twice in the early evening, as Posey lay looking up at the restless leaves, and wondering in torment what had become of old grizzly's sister, he imagained he heard a voice from the high rim above. A soft voice calling his name! He jumped with a start. At that second a mourning dove flew from the shelf of the ledge and Posey gave it credit for what had seemed to be—possibly—the pleading voice of little sister.

Yet, after that, in the dark hours of the night when all doves were asleep, something on that strange cliff-brow roused Posey from his dreams. He sat up with a great start to listen. It was still night. He was wide awake. Yet from that lofty rim he heard his name— it was Toorah's voice! She called him twice.

"*O aakerom!*" (Yes!) he shouted, springing to his feet. "Where are you?"

"Come and get me!" she called in great excitement seemingly in muffled voice, yet speaking as plainly and as unmistakably as ever he had heard her speak.

"I am coming! I am coming!" he shouted back through the darkness while running from under the trees to gaze frantically at the huge rock towering above him. He cudgled his brain to think of some place he had seen where he might climb up, but the great cliff was vague and dark. He stumbled over brush and stones as he rushed along trying to keep his eyes on the place from whence the voice came.

"Where are you?" he called again, raising his voice. No answer came. He called again, listening with his whole being, but he heard only his throbbing heart and the rising and falling of a little breeze that moaned over the cliff and through the tree-tops. Though he called again and still again, he could hear nothing else. Silence mocked at his voice in the hush of night.

Toorah was dead! It was her lovely spirit that had called to him from the hereafter.

Sleep was miles and miles away from Posey. He groped his way along the vertical wall and into a little canyon. The gray dawn revealed a way in which he might climb to the clifftop. Getting over it, fingers and toes, with all possible speed, he hurried over to the brow above his wickiup.

Most of the region near the rim was sandrock, bare and smooth. Yet, in a little depression where the sand had been drifted in by the wind, he found the imprint of a woman's moccasined feet—Toorah's feet? Who knew? Why should a woman be there? Whoever it was had been running. Farther on he found the track again—it had been made in desperate haste. Still he found it again and on it a big track—the track of a man!

Posey bent searchingly over every trace of activity, hunting far out from the rim, trying to make out what had happened. He found the mark of horses' feet, but they seemed to go nowhere in particular, and were lost in the beaten trails.

Maybe Toorah was not dead. Maybe she had been hunting him, and some man who had bought her was dragging her away. Could that be? O she was far away! She was never real any more. Surely she was dead. In his long and desperate hunt for a will-o-the-wisp Posey had lost his reason. The tracks he had seemed to see and the voice he had seemed to hear might have their existence nowhere but in his over-wrought brain.

CHAPTER TEN

TOOISH APANE!

A bitter quarrel flared up between Paddy and his cousin, Neepooch Grasshopper. Neepooch had robbed the Mormons until he found them guarding everything day and night. Then he turned to prey on some of his own people. Paddy, being recently left fatherless, Neepooch took him for easy prey.

Paddy was by nature a greater soul than the run of his tribe. Fearless without boasting, he wanted to treat everybody right and live in peace. Paiute though he was, he maintained a creditable standard of honor through all the troubled years of his rather short life. He generously forgave his cousin the first time and the second time, but when Neepooch stole his horses the third time and spurned all offers of peace, and struck Paddy with a heavy club leaving him for dead, Paddy took his gun and declared war to the death.

Old Pee-age, well known and much loved by the people of Bluff, was grandmother to both the boys. From the time of Paddy's birth she lived with Paddy's mother, and Paddy seemed like her very own child. On the other hand, Neepooch, son of another daughter, was quite a stranger.

The two cousins hunted one another up and down with rising wrath. Paddy's mother and grandmother paced back and forth in great anxiety day and night, or lay awake by their dim fire dreading what might be happening to their boy. Sometimes he rode in suddenly on the lope, snatched a bite of something to eat, got a fresh horse and was gone. They knew not where.

In his fury Paddy swore he would never stop till he
had killed Neepooch. Likewise Neepooch swore he
would go till he killed Paddy.

Sometimes the two women saw nothing of their
young brave for days and weeks at a time. They grew
wild with anguish, fearing he would never come back.

The Paiute way, when two of their tribe get to
fighting, whether man with man, or man with woman,
is to let them carry the conflict to a finish without
outside interference. Relatives of the unfortunate one
may take severe reprisals after the fight is over, but
they must refrain while it is in progress. The whole
tribe knew the two boys had begun a death duel,
but the hands-off policy prevented anyone from taking
part.

The long torturing days had passed since the
waiting mother and grandmother heard a word from
their fighting brave. He might be at Navaho Mountain
a hundred miles to the west, or he might be in the Ute
reservation more than a hundred miles in the opposite
direction. He might be in the maze of unfrequented
wilderness beyond Wooden Shoe buttes, or— he might
be lying in his blood where Neepooch Grasshopper had
overpowered him.

The two women had their camp hidden in a fork
of Spring Canyon where Paddy could come to them
without being seen. The Chee-poots people still were
camped where they had moved near the mouth of
Cottonwood. In her desperation, old Pee-age, started
down through the two miles of greasewood to hear what
she could from old Chee-poots or any of his household.

Afoot, slow and sorrowing, she met Posey headed
for Tank Bench. He rode by without a word, although
she was trying with her cracked old voice to speak to

him. Then she called to him, imploring him to wait and listen. He knew what she wanted; he would not borrow trouble by seeming to take any part in the death-duel between her grandsons. She was crying. Her withered old croak reached its capacity and was growing dim behind him when he heard her speak the name of Toorah.

He reined his horse at once— he listened—he turned back and asked her what she said. She was quoting Paddy: In his long chase over the country, reaching from Moencopy in Arizona, through San Juan in Utah to Pine River in Colorado, he had seen Toorah. He didn't say where he had seen her, but he mentioned seeing her. Now if Posey would hunt him up, take him a fresh horse and something to eat, he could tell Posey where the little sister had gone.

Posey agreed at once to try. The old woman was never to tell a thing about it, and Posey was to let her know as soon as he found her boy. Getting a fresh mount he went from camp to camp, concealing his real purpose as he had become expert in doing. Yet he tried by every sly device to pick up any possible clue that would lead him to the fighting grandson of old Pee-age.

Until now he had cared nothing about which of the two cousins survived. Now it was suddenly of terrible importance. If Paddy were killed before they met, he might miss his life-chance of finding out what he wanted most of all things to know! He would get that information even if he had to waylay Grasshopper himself.

Someone had seen Paddy on a jaded horse in Mc-Elmo Canyon. Straight for that point Posey raced. After much sly inquiry he followed another tip on to Merriano Springs. Hearing that Grasshopper had been seen on the San Juan south of there, Posey hurried with his fresh horse and sack of refreshments to the river. He followed doubtful clues to Bluff, forty miles to the west, eating up day after day in his search, but unflagging in his determination.

He ascertained definitely that the two feuding cousins had been seen near Moencopy in distant Arizona. He departed thither as soon as his horses were able to go. After losing four days sniffing old trails in the Navaho reservation, he got a hot tip which sent him flying northeast toward Bluff.

This racing back and forth over a territory three hundred miles in extent, imposed unusual necessities on these fighting cousins. With their lives at stake they had to meet these necessities, even if they got that supply by taking it at gun point. When the murder-sworn enemy came nearer and nearer behind, and the whole fight was about to be lost for the sake of a fresh horse, any fresh horse within reach was immediately requisitioned even if it carried its master on its back, and the exhausted animal was left in its place.

Food, drink, beds and concealment were likewise taken over, generally by promise of due reward at some future time.

These fighting cousins mastered the secret of meeting desperate emergencies. Over the wide range of their battlefield they traveled on a motley and extemporaneous relay of ponies, accomplishing each change in about the time it takes to transfer a saddle from one horse to another.

The sudden appearance of one or the other of these desperate fighters at a camp or herd, brought quick excitement and sharp activity till he loped away on a fresh horse, leaving his panting, lathered cayuse behind. Sometimes the pursuer found the horse of the pursued sufficiently rested to carry him on in the chase.

The offensive was taken first by one and then by the other. The problem was always to dodge an ambush, to spring a deadly surprise, or to find the other on a jaded horse. Survival was a matter of fresh horses, keen wits, good guns, and a full belly.

Late one afternoon, hatless and wearing a torn red shirt, Neepooch Grasshopper came riding into Bluff from the west, his cayuse wet with lather and scarred with the lash. Whip and spur, he urged the drooping creature on up the road towards Recapture.

The clatter of hoofs had no more than died in the distance when Paddy loped in on the hot trail, his pony wet but making good time. He too disappeared towards Recapture, his gun across his saddle in front of him.

Half an hour later, Posey appeared on the tracks from the west and followed them off to the east. On the sandhills north of the Jump, Posey met Paddy coming back. He was leading a pony with an empty saddle and a gun hanging on the side. He rode slowly and at ease, his own gun in its scabbard under the fender. He was headed for the hidden camp in Spring Canyon four miles away where he would make his own report to the anxious women, relieving Posey of that responsibility, and also depriving Posey of any bargaining wedge.

Ten days after that race through Bluff, a boy was herding sheep near the mouth of Recapture. His attention was attracted to a strange heap of stones. Pulling them down he uncovered the body of an Indian wearing a torn red shirt. The dead face showed powder-burns and a gaping bullet-hole in the center of the fore-head.

When Posey met his long-sought man, he knew the fight was over. He knew too, from the grim visage before him, that no spying or prying would be tolerated for one minute.

"Impo ashanty?" (What do you want?) Paddy de-manded in uncompromising tones.

Posey told about meeting old Pee-age in the grease-woods, and of following the crooked trail to Merriano Springs and through the reservation with a fresh horse and provisions. No, he was not spying. He didn't expect to tell a word about it. But he did want to know —he wanted most of all to know the thing about which Paddy had told his mother and grandmother— he had mentioned to them that somewhere in his travels he had seen Poke's little sister. Would Paddy just say where she could be found? Posey would never betray the source of this information.

Paddy didn't know where she was.

What? Hadn't he seen her? Old Pee-age declared he had seen her.

O, that was weeks ago, and that camp was due to move right away.

Well, where was it? Where was that camp?

It would do Posey no good to know—one of her brothers guarded her all the time.

Guarded her? well where? Even if the camp had moved—where had it moved from? Where in the world had he seen Toorah?

He had seen her in a camp hidden in the big cedars near Paiute Springs.

It was eighty miles to Paiute Springs. Posey's quick impulse was to start at once, but he must return to the mouth of Cottonwood for fresh horses. By the open roads and trails it was eighty miles to the Springs, but it would not do to travel in the open, nor in the day-time. He would have to go over unfrequented trails under cover of night.

He took with him an extra horse and saddle, concealing that extra saddle under a light pack. He reached the neighborhood of the springs in the dark hours just before dawn. Quiet reigned in the forest of big cedars. No dog barked. No smell of smoke was in the air. With the first rays of light Posey moved cautiously about looking for tracks, listening for sounds. They had gone!

For a long time Posey tried desperately to determine which direction they had gone. It seemed hopeless. Utterly hopeless! Since it was summertime they had dragged no tent-poles to leave a lasting mark. More confusing still, Posey had reason to think they might have started Paiute-style, in the opposite direction from which they intended to go, if only to confuse whoever might try to follow them.

All the same, this being his very first clue, he must trace it to them even though it took the rest of the summer. After hunting around there most of the forenoon, he met a cowpuncher named King.

"Where's Paiute camp?" he asked eagerly.

"No sabey," King answered indifferently.

"You seeum this camp over here?"

"I saw no smoke."

"How many days go?" Posey pursued.

King indicated with his fingers that they had left about ten days before.

"You seeum go?"

"Over here me seeum trail," the cowboy motioned towards Blue Mountain. Then becoming more interested and ready to speak, he admitted he had met them.

Posey listened with open mouth. "How many?"

"No sabey, maybeso ten."

"How many squaws?"

"I don't know—one squaw all same here," and King held together his wrists indicating that one of the squaws had her wrists tied with a rope.

Posey leaned forward with wide eyes, "What's a matter rope?" he demanded, lost in the vision inspired by King's words.

"Injun talk, squaw all time run away," the cowpuncher explained. "Talk, five days huntum—rope pixum—(fixem) no more run away."

Fury and resolution boiling through his veins, Posey headed for the west, avoiding the trail wherever he could. He began to understand: Toorah had tried to get away—she had been gone five days. She had tried in the darkness to find him. When she hunted along the rim and called for him, they had heard her, found her and taken her back. Now she was hobbled like a horse.

In spite of his care to keep out of sight, he met another white man near Peter's Point. He learned that some Indians were camped near the spring. Hiding his horse in the brush half a mile away Posey crept in ever so carefully to spy out the situation.

But that camp, near the ledge and trees, was not hidden at all. It could be plainly seen from the wagon-road across the canyon. Three saddled horses waited near it under a tree. By the sound Posey knew that a big game of *ducki* occupied all the Indians there in one wickiup.

He crept nearer. The big lure of those cards, and the values staked on their colors, entranced that wickiup-full of people with hypnotic grip. They quarreled with rising emphasis, each one trying to make himself heard above the others.

"You lie!" roared a familiar voice. Where had Posey heard that voice before? O yes! It was one of Old Rooster's sons whom he had met on Pine River when he hunted there for little sister.

By the time he recognized the voice of Rooster's second son—more strong language— and threatening words. Then, as he listened with bated breath, he heard an unmistakable grunt which might have said, *Pu-neeh.* Old grizzly Poke was in the game! As he harked further, he heard Hatch, and then Bishop's rasping voice. He listened in vain for a sound from the fourth brother, Teegre. Where was he?

Something in the *ducki* game, fast and furious, something with rising wrath and menacing import, filled him with sharp eagerness to go and see how it would terminate. It seemed quite impossible that such a heated contest could cool off without an explosion.

It was hard to guess what all this could mean. The camp in plain sight and all present embroiled in a game of *ducki*. Surely the little sister was not here. They would not have her in a camp by the public highway. He could see what appeared to be all the squaws crowded in the doorway of the *ducki* wickiup, craning their necks to watch the players.

An idea struck Posey— a wonderful idea. He listened again and still failed to hear the voice of Teegre. If Teegre were there he was silent, which meant he was not there. Anyway, there were only three ponies tied under the tree. Toorah's three brothers had come in from their hidden camp to this camp of the Rooster brothers.

Posey crept back to his horse and began making a big circle looking for tracks, still hindered by the danger of getting too much in sight. He bent low towards the ground as he rode. No marks in the dust escaped his sharp eyes. He stopped short —three horses had come in from the thick cedar country on the point to the north.

With eager haste he traced those three tracks back toward the larger and more dense growth of timber on the point. Three miles away, in quite a jungle of trees and brush, a dog barked somewhere ahead of him. He stopped with his horses to listen. What should he do? It was late afternoon. Without doubt this was the place he had been hunting for endless months. Toorah was a prisoner! Teegre was almost sure to be on guard. Still it might be that the squaws were thought equal to the task since the run-away was bound.

At all events, grizzly old Poke was not there with his terrible hogstring. But he would come. He and his brothers! The darkness would be more perilous than the day in escaping them.

Moving his horses from that secret trail, Posey hid them in the brush and crept in to spy on the camp. Spying on a hundred camps in the past year had made him an expert.

That dog continued to bark. Other dogs joined in as if they would come out and advertise his presence.

The only way to quiet them would be to withdraw or
stop still; otherwise he would have to go in boldly and
face them.

Teegre might be there, or the wife of the dread
grizzly might be the only guard. No difference. Posey
was determined enough now to face the old grizzly
with his hogstring. This was a tremendous moment—
the supreme moment of years. Assuring himself of
his pistol and his knife on his hip, he marched straight
for Old Grizzly's den.

Three yellow dogs met him halfway. He fought
them off till he stopped in surprise at the very door of
the wickiup. There in the rude entrance to her abode,
stood Poke's squaw, waiting to see what kind of
animal had aroused the dogs.

"Pu-neeh!" she shrieked in fury and amazement,
urging the yellow curs to drive him away.

Quick behind her Toorah appeared trying to come
out. Toorah ordered the dogs to come back. Crowding
out through the opening she tried to reach them with
a stick, but her hands were tied and she made poor
headway. She had advanced well out into the doorway when the older woman seized her and tried to
drag her back.

"*Posey, tooish apane!*" (hurry!) she called in the
urgency of one combined word, turning her face ap-
pealingly towards him.

Spurred by her plea Posey kicked the dogs right
and left. With his knife ready in his hand he stabbed
one of the furies in the side and leaped to the struggling
women. Two of the dogs attacked him again. He
tripped over one of them and fell. All the time he was
vaguely aware of someone calling and coming from

a near-by camp. On his feet again he sank his knife
into the second snarling dog and snatched Toorah
from her determined sister-in-law. He slashed the
rope on her wrists and turned to fend himself from
Mrs. Poke or the dogs or whoever was coming.

Toorah gripped his hand as she had done at Navaho Mountain, pulling him away. *"Tooish apane!"*
(Hurry!) she panted. "Teegre!" Wildly she pulled
him in the direction from which he had come. They
must hurry! Teegre was very near.

Holding firmly to her soft hand, Posey almost
dragged her after him between trees and through
a maze of brush to his waiting horses. This seemed a
continuation of that wonderful dash they began to
make together in the thicket of birch willows at La
Sal. Years of waiting and hoping and hunting had
deferred their hope till now it was intensified a
thousandfold.

Panting and eager and thrilled to the very finger-
tips, they reached the horses. As Posey boosted Toorah
to one of the saddles and he sprang to the other, someone came crashing through the brush behind them.

Posey struck a lope on the first jump and Toorah
rode close behind. Over rocks, down banks, through
brush, they made a desperate scramble to put distance
between themselves and that howling camp behind.
They must reach the mountain and the tall timber.
But the camp of the Rooster boys and the big *ducki*
game lay squarely in their way. To miss it they would
have to cross the rugged canyon instead of following
the trail around its head.

"Does Teegre have a horse?" demanded Posey.

"No, but he will soon get one," replied the breathless Toorah.

He would warn Poke, then the four brothers would follow with lightning fury.

Posey led the way down a cedar-grown swale. Desperately they looked for a place to get off the rim into Peter's canyon. The edge dropped abruptly before them. No way to go.

Into the anxious hush of their tense pause broke an ominous sound: hoofs— beating hoofs, crashing madly towards them. The thick cedars hid the frantic couple from view on the east, but their only escape seemed to be to plunge down a fifty-foot wall. Toorah snatched Posey's pistol from its holster. *"Tooish apane!"* she breathed in a loud whisper, motioning him to have his rifle ready.

The pounding hoofs came smashing through dry limbs, over brush, over rocks, neck or nothing. The murderous whack of whips mingled with panting of horses straining to the bursting point of exertion.

With bated breath and guns cocked, Posey and Toorah caught glimpses through the trees of Poke and Bishop riding as from the devil himself, too intent on looking ahead to take one look right or left. On they crashed into the forest—on out of sight. Their sound became dim and died away in the distance.

The run-aways found a place to get their horses down the high rim in the least possible time. They crossed to the west side of the canyon. Straight for the tall timber Posey raced with Toorah riding devotedly near behind. Her hostile brothers might find their tracks, but they would not be able to follow them. In the field of grass and flowers among the tall timber ahead, no clue would be left to indicate where they had gone. In front of the fleeing lovers rose the great

friendly mountain — blessed freedom— and the sheltering arm of night.

Posey told Toorah they would not go to Navaho
Mountain; her people would be sure to search there
first. Instead they would hide in the wild country beyond the Wooden Shoe buttes. No one would think of
going there after them.

Daylight again found them deeply hidden in the
wooded north slope of Blue Mountain. Their trail
through the grass would elude anything less than a
bloodhound. Wonderful days followed. Whether clouds
or sunshine they took their course by easy steps through
the most remote regions and chose a resting place
in a canyon beyond Deer Flat west of Wooden Shoes.
It was the limit of remoteness and security, a wild
Eden of bliss.

In their solitary paradise they gave no thought
to her people nor to his. Why should they? Their world
was quite complete. Just the two of them. They were
the supreme rulers of this wilderness. Together they
hunted deer and gathered fat pods of the big yucca.
They found plenty to eat and abundance of grass.

Their canyon had but one place where a horse could
get in or out. By laying a dry limb across that entrance,
they converted the place into a closed pasture. Some
days they didn't so much as bother to saddle their
horses, or leave the green shade where they had made
their camp. Still they liked to ride frequently back
across Deer Flat and look from Wooden Shoes for
any indication of life on the mountain.

One morning as they rode up to the entrance of
their canyon pasture they found tracks! Tracks of
ponies other than their own. They found the print
of a man's moccasined foot. Two men! Careful

examination of the tracks showed that they were made
by Paiute moccasins.

Two men had gone down the canyon and might
even now be by the fire in the little sanctuary. They
slowed down to a standstill and examined the tracks
with uneasy surprise. No mistake. Two men had been
there just a few minutes before. From bending over
those unwelcome tracks in the dust, they listened with
bated breath, only to hear the wind sighing through
the trees on the hillside.

Why had they not met those prowlers? Surely some
hidden evil was plotting and skulking around them.
No telling who it might be. No telling what cruel
advantage the intruders might have in their hands.
Posey and his bride would fly from the canyon—fly
anywhere before it was too late. They whipped up to a
lope, but at the foot of the hill they heard something
like a voice above them.

That voice-sound came again, giving them a cold
and creepy sensation. Then they discovered that someone was hiding behind a tree near the trail, someone
who was making sure they did not get out of the
canyon.

Toorah seized Posey's pistol and motioned him to
be ready with his gun. It was a foolish hope; to raise
their guns there in the open would be inviting a dead
shot from cover, possibly to hit them in the back.

They paused in vexed bewilderment. "Let's go
back," she suggested, her black eyes the more beautiful
for the sparkle of anger and anguish she felt.

With their first move to turn back down the
canyon, a familiar voice called from that tree above
them ordering them to stop. At the same time they

heard another voice below—or was it an echo? They waited—no escape. From behind that tree came a sombre form with a wide black hat and a vertical inky mustache hiding his mouth. He descended the hill slowly towards them.

"Pu-neeh!" he grunted. "You sneaked in there when I was away." He carried his gun in his hand but showed no intention of using it. Surely he had someone with him or he would not venture so carelessly towards them. "If I had been there, you would have been treated like the sneaking coyote you are. Now I have you in a trap."

"Trapped coyotes can bite," hissed his sister, half raising the pistol in her hand.

"Don't be a fool," he grunted, showing no concern for the gun she held, yet sounding in some way as if he were carrying a deep sorrow.

"What has he done?" she snapped, "that you want to kill him like a coyote in a trap?" As she lowered the pistol she glanced from side to side trying to discover his hidden confederate. "Am I your horse that you must keep me hobbled and guarded? When I get away you trail me up and want to drag me back like a slave! Now, like an old bear you are after me again."

Poke met her fury with stony silence. He seemed to be almost sympathetic. They could not understand it. Still Toorah glared at him in hot resentment, being thoroughly aroused, and refraining from using the gun in her hand only through fear of some one else shooting her in the back.

"Kill us!" she cursed with clenched teeth. "Kill both of us!" She faced him defiantly as a game little animal crowded to the wall.

Still strangely unruffled, and bearing a look as of some deeper emotion, the old bear regarded his baby sister thoughtfully. "I didn't follow you," he declared. "I didn't expect to see you—didn't know till this morning you were here."

"Didn't follow us? Then why are you here talking of killing us like coyotes in a trap?" she demanded.

"Listen," and still he was not angered, "a bad, bad thing has happened."

Then he related the tragedy which ever since that time has been written as a red paragraph in the history of San Juan county. It happened about the time that Posey found the hidden camp in the cedars. It happened in the big *ducki* game in the Rooster wick-iup near Peter's Spring. A fierce quarrel developed, Posey heard the beginning of it, but as it rose in fury, the Rooster Brothers killed Hatch. Then Poke and Bishop killed the Rooster brothers. Old Rooster and his friends, wild for revenge, pursued Poke and Bishop as they fled for their lives. In their wild dash they had almost run over Posey and Toorah without knowing it. Barely touching at their camp in their flight, and having no time to do anything about the elopers, they had fled for the remote quarters west of Wooden Shoes as the safest place to hide.

Before Poke quit talking, Bishop came up from below with the two horses. He waited while Poke answered Toorah's questions about the killing.

Turning to Posey the old bear's face took on its grizzly aspect again. "Skunk! Renegade pup!" he grunted in aversion, "but it happens to be a good thing for me that you are here. I'll give you a chance on one condition."

Then he demanded ten horses in payment for his sister, ten horses broken to ride. And Posey was to return with flour, bacon, and other stipulated items of food to the hangout in the canyon. He was also to find out and report conditions on the outside, especially what old man Rooster and his friends were doing.

Posey accepted without argument. When Poke stepped aside and motioned the couple up the trail, they went promptly.

Victory again! The trouble had really turned out right after all, just as Haskel had said. Also, in accord with the old white man's medicine, Hatch, the persistent horse-thief was dead. Tuvagutts and Bob and others who came under the ban, had been nailed by some of the evil agencies Haskel had predicted.

What were ten horses in a country with plenty of horses? And what was the price of a grub-stake and a few trips back to the hangout west of Deer Flat? The skunk would win the old bear's everlasting favor by doing the job ten times better than he was expected to do it.

Straight over the main trail and in broad daylight he headed with his bride for the home camp at the mouth of Cottonwood. This marked the dawn of a new era in Posey's life. A happy golden era too good to last.

The proud moment of his victorious arrival with Toorah at his old father's wickiup, was a bright day in Posey's life never to be forgotten. It was a memory to amplify the sting of changed conditions in the distracted years ahead.

Posey filled Poke's orders to the last trifling particular. In addition he added sweets and other pleasurable things, bidding for favor by bringing cheer to the old grizzly while his exile lasted. Posey also delivered the stipulated number of horses, guaranteeing to make good any one of them which might happen to be replevied (reclaimed by the sheriff), a weakness to which be knew that every one of the animals was subject.

CHAPTER ELEVEN

BIG-MOUTH MIKE

The barriers of Poke's exile crumbled away, and Paiute life settled down to a normalcy somewhat new. Hatch was gone. Sanop had sickened and died. One of his incorrigible sons languished in a jail in Cortez, Colorado. The other hid somewhere in the rocks of Ute Mountain sought by a dozen deadly enemies.

Posey's sudden change of fortune left in him no inclination to humility, even though he had observed the strange way in which Haskel's words came true. Disaster or death had seemed to select the two leading thieves, Posey couldn't fail to see that. The first reports of it had been sharply impressive, but now, plump and secure, Posey reasoned that is how it would have happened anyway. Nothing in it about which to be disturbed.

The important thing about it all was that his own heavy burden of sorrow had been lifted. Toorah was his devoted shadow wherever he went. Her dreaded brother had been pacified. Life was bright—like a bright morning after the storm—why worry?

Toorah was really his own! The thought of it lifted Posey in a wild transport of delight. The little sister of the invincible cavalier—the spirit of his dreams—she had come back from the mists and the maze to his own wickiup. Her voice which he had heard in sorrow on the desert winds in the midnight, was the real voice of the girl who clung to him and loved him. He was a victor, a king. He had come into his own splendid heritage.

Through optimistic eyes he saw his luck about to change for the better in everything. Unfortunately for him at this particular time he won three horses from his darling enemy, Bitseel, in a glorious whirl of *ducki*. Three horses taken with imperial hand from the despised Navaho. With them and four Mormon horses he intended to take from near the mouth of Recapture, he would be well towards recovery from the ten he had had to deliver to Poke.

When he went to nail those four saddlers near the mouth of Recapture, he found only a hot trail leading across the river to the hogan of Bitseel. The Navaho had stolen the four horses to balance his accounts after Posey had trimmed him at *ducki*. This was a troublesome fly in Posey's ointment. He grieved over it. It was a bad omen in his honeymoon. Also it was a great injustice to the poor man in Bluff who was depending on those horses for a livelihood. With a suddenly aroused sense of propriety and justice, Posey went to Bluff and kindly informed the owner of the horses where they had gone.

Bishop Nielson sent Haskel across the river to recover the much-needed animals. After a long, tiresome hunt the old man brought them back. The owner, delighted to see them again, put them in a secluded grassy canyon to be refreshed for important work soon to be done. It was Posey's business and profession to spy on the whole process. He forthwith went to that grassy canyon and corrected the whole complication of untoward events by applying the four horses to the improvement of his own status as he had first intended.

Somebody told Bitseel that the despised Posey had given him away and spoiled his rich haul from near Recapture. *"Chinde! Cliz! Cliz!"* he hissed, and set

himself and some of his people to spy on the Chee-poots
people for an opening to even the score with compound
interest. Posey knew nothing of this damaging report
having been taken to his enemy, and made no pro-
vision to repel new hostilities.

Posey's people bought a fine stallion. They had
wanted it for a long time, and having no way to get
it by stealth, they paid a good price for it, intending
to raise fine horses of their very own. The big Navaho
took smiling account of this handsome creature, and
of the fond expectations of its unsuspecting owners.

Somewhere behind a bank of black clouds the sun
was setting. A damp breath of approaching storm
whispered from the southwest. In the dusk the big
Navaho waited on his invincible sorrel pony, peering
intently over a ridge at a dozen horses on the sandhills below. The darkness thickened. Big drops of cold
water splashed the dust. Now was his chance! Bitseel
raised his quirt and loped cautiously down the shallow
ravine. Bending low in the saddle after driving the
horses over against a high bank he lassoed the pinto
stallion, keeping all the while his sharp eyes leveled
on the wickiups in the canyon below. As the rain
descended in a roar all around, he rode at furious
gallop to the ford of the San Juan, leading the unwilling pinto behind him.

When bright morning beamed again on a wet world
washed clean of all tracks, the handsome pinto cropped
the grass in a remote valley of the reservation.
At the same time a boy from the Chee-poots camp
returned to relate that the fine peechoogy (stallion)
was nowhere to be found. The much-priced *peechoogy*
secured at such a fancy price and so carefully cared
for, to sire a lot of choice colts—gone! Hot indignation
spread through the camp.

Posey knew the stallion had not parted of its own will from the other horses. Whose will then? Unaware that his act of kindness to that man in Bluff was known and had thrown oil on the flame of his old quarrel, he couldn't quite focus on Bitseel as the author of this latest calamity. Later in the summer a friend returning from the reservation, told him what had become of the valuable horse. His hatred burned with acid fury day and night plotting revenge.

He knew the big Navaho cherished his invincible sorrel, and a perfect darling of a bay, a single-footer with white "socks" on all four feet. During many a long game of *coocan* back of the old log store in Bluff, one or the other of these two beauties stood waiting by the old bull fence. In person or by proxy Posey shadowed the stocking-footer and the sorrel till he knew just where to find them at any set hour.

There are times on the San Juan wilderness when a moaning south-western fills the sky with dust and drives coarse sand as if it were fine shot against every open surface. In such a storm men and animals, unless they are goaded on by urgent necessity, seek a place of shelter.

On such a day when a man could see ahead of him barely five rods if he could keep his eyes open at all, Posey rode fast and far in a hail of sharp grit. At a gravel ford a mile below the old rock house he splashed into the river. On the south side he struck a lope again and headed into a greasewood canyon, scornful of the stinging sand.

Blinding clouds of dust hid Bitseel's hogan half a mile below. Even though he could not see it, Posey knew exactly where it stood. Keeping vigilant watch he raced in that direction. Fifteen minutes later he came out of that canyon leading the sorrel and the

stocking-footer. At mad gait he whipped back to the
gravel ford. Reaching the north side in safety, he
spurned all beaten trails and disappeared into the hills.

Months passed before these devoted adversaries
met again — months of chuckling exultation for the
thief on the north side of the river and months of
bitter cursing for the thief on the south.

In remote corners a hundred miles to the west of
Bluff, the Mormons tried to hide a few stock horses.
With them they had frequently put saddle horses
needing a rest. These places had a special attraction
for Posey and his people. They stole horses from Clay
Hill, from Red Canyon, from the Cow Tank, and
from Elk Mountain. They stole from Comb Wash,
from the Valley of the Butler, and from under the
very noses of the people in town. Posey kept an
up-to-the-minute directory of all Bluff's horses with
a record of the dates they would be free to receive
attention.

Of such an intolerable nuisance as this, Haskel
could not fail to take thoughtful account. Going to
the Chee-poots wickiups in Cow Canyon, he addressed
himself to Posey in particular, fixing his black eyes
on the enterprising horse-thief with prophetic pen-
etration.

"Are the things true that I have told you?" he
began, as of with full authority to call for an accounting. Smitten with unaccustomed feelings of guilt
Posey tried to evade an answer and hung his head.
"You know these things are true," pursued the old
man firmly. "In what one thing have my words to
you failed? Most of the thieves are dead. One of
Sanop's boys died in jail, and the other like a coyote
among the rocks of Ute Mountain. Buck Grasshopper

is stealing from Poke, and Poke will kill him. *Shin-op*
pities us, and if you go on stealing from us, you will
die the same as the other thieves."

Posey listened sullenly like a whipped cur under
the lash. Toorah, her baby at her breast, her ebony
hair parted neatly in the middle, frowned her resentment for this scathing arraignment of her lord. Old
Chee-poots, more weak than wicked, was troubled
and oppressed. Then without another word the old
gray-beard turned and left the wickiup.

That visit resulted in a temporary lull in Posey's
operations—a lull and nothing more. He studied it
over, uncomfortably recalling every word the old man
had said.

While he still pondered, and hesitated, and half
feared, some of his people reported the approach of
a hundred Navahos. Armed and daubed with war-
paint, they intended to massacre the people of Bluff,
and burn every house. Misinformed and inflamed over
some trouble at Rincone, involving a Bluff man and
a dead Navaho, some had sworn vengeance on the little
settlement, intending a surprise attack.

The Paiutes knew Haskel had left town on
business, so one of them suggested—not so much from
curiosity as from exultant contempt—"Let's go and
see how Shin-op fights these hundred Navahos to
protect the people he pities."

When that terrible cavalcade, like Atilla's invincible horde, came riding into the defenseless town of
Bluff, the Chee-poots people rode in behind them.
With glittering ornaments and jingling silver buckles
the long procession stopped in dreadful array their
guns across their saddles, in front of the old log store.
They demanded to see the bishop, or some other re-

presentative man. He must account to them for charges they had come to make against the people of Bluff.

Most of the men of the settlement had gone freighting, or were on the range, or were hunting stolen stock, or pursuing other various labors many miles away. Only three men remained in town, for no one had expected trouble like this. Terrified women and children peeped through the darkened windows or ran to their neighbors in dismay.

Someone hurried to Bishop Nielson, an aged patriarch from Denmark, whose hair was white, and whose feet had been frozen crooked in the famous handcart tragedy on the plains. The old man came limping along to meet the hostile band. Upon reaching them he found his faithful interpreter there, Kumen Jones, who was able to speak to the Navahos in their own language.

The Chee-poots people watched with interest. Haskel might be able to cope with this situation, but this aged Dane wouldn't have a chance! Hardly able to speak English, he would get nowhere with these infuriated Navaho hornets. The Paiutes watched the old bishop calmly tell his interpreter what to say. The painted Navahos showed their annoyance at his fearless demeanor.

"We came here to be your friends," began the bishop as if it might have been Haskel himself. "It is not our business to fight, the Great Spirit sent us here to teach you the ways of peace. If you want to fight, we will make it known to the government and they will have soldiers here right away. Do you want to be our friends, or shall we send word to the government to start a war?"

"*Doetah! Doetah!*" (No! No!) objected the older men, raising their hands in protest. The very suggestion roused unpleasant recollections of Kit Carson and his terrible men who took them away as cattle in a great herd to the bull-pen in New Mexico. Most of the Navahos in that mob were too young to remember the humiliations of the three years in Bosque Redondo, and they sat sullenly on their horses.

"All you who want to be our friends and live in peace," the bishop went on speaking through Kumen Jones, "go stand your guns against the wall of the store, and come and sit here in a friendly circle while we talk it over."

The older men leaned their guns against the wall and seated themselves on the ground. The young hot-heads remained stiffly on their horses. The Chee-poots people watched to see how *Shin-op* took part. The conversation on the ground was too low for the men on the horses to hear. One by one they stacked their long fire-arms and drew near to the white men on the ground to find out what was being said. Then the Paiutes got down where they could hear what was going on. They saw, with surprise and disappointment, that the angry braves with blackened faces yielded to the old bishop's standards of peace and good will. Soon the Paiutes, like the fool who came to scoff but remained to pray, agreed with the hearty accord which won them all like a strain of music.

Especially did the Paiutes agree when after the big handshake all around, the bishop announced they would kill a fat steer and bring bacon and flour and coffee out of the store for a generous feed that night and the next morning, in order that all who had come so far and were so weary could go home refreshed.

The Chee-poots people ate as freely as anyone else, and they heard—even though they may not have

taken part in it—all the heartfelt pledges of friendship between the Mormons and the Navahos.

Could these Paiutes forget that impressive scene?
Could Posey really cast free from his mind all the
fervent words and friendly assurances of good will?
How different would be the ending of this story if he
had treasured in his heart the words of good will he
heard on that occasion.

*   *   *   *   *

Old Big-Mouth Mike, insolent and contriving, suddenly became a wool-merchant. Every day he came
from the direction of the reservation with a back-load
of wool which he sold to the little store. After paying
for it, the clerk dumped it in one of the back rooms of
the log building, but somehow, many purchases of
wool from Big-Mouth Mike failed to increase the pile
of wool in the back room.

Lem Redd, the store superintendent, investigated
and set a huge wolf-trap under a loose chink in the
wall of that back room. In the morning Big-Mouth
Mike stood there by the wall with his arm through
the place of the big chink, his hand in the trap. When
Lem Redd came to the store he took the old chief by the
hair, and brought the toe of his boot in violent contact
with the seat of Mike's breeches, pointing out in strong
language the impropriety of selling wool in the day-
time and stealing it back at night. When Mike had
been well kicked and properly informed as to what
kind of a yellow dog he was, the superintendent went
inside the warehouse and released the swollen fingers
from the hard and biting jaws of the trap.

Big-Mouth had very little to say while he received
the kicking, and he had no answering comment to the
lecture on the folly of wrong-doing, yet while he nursed

his sore hand in the quiet of his wickiup, he
awoke to the enormity of the outrage he had suffered. He, who had killed a white man as flippantly
as he would kill a goat—he, who got away with
plunder slick and clean, now to be kicked and insulted
by a white man without a gun.

When his old followers came to his wickiup to look
with a suppressed smile at their kicked chief, he
became a roaring lion. "Wait till you see how much I
make them pay for this indignity," he growled. "They
can't do this to me!"

It was simply more than his proud soul would
bear. With dark and terrible visage he stalked into
Bluff demanding a thousand dollars indemnity. The
money must be forth-coming at once or he would make
the little colony a waste of blood and ashes.

Mike! the terror of the wilderness! The terrible
killer boasting of the blood on his hands. Mike! the
dread of any white woman or child who ventured
beyond the narrow limits of the remote little town.
From their windows the settlers peeped, watching anxiously to see whether he would turn toward their door
or go on by.

With the lips of his long wide mouth protruding
to advertise his awful displeasure, he met Haskel on
the street. Determined by the heat of his rancor and
the noise of his words to dominate the old man's sentiments, he poured forth his wrath in threats and
curses. He had been outraged! He demanded a thousand dollars in silver. If payment were delayed, something terrible would happen.

The Mormon medicine man stared at the ground,
annoyed at being detained, but otherwise uncon-

cerned as if a spoiled child had begun to whine after him.

When at length Mike closed his ponderous yap, eager to know how much of a dent he had made in the old man's armor, Haskel turned on him without the least emotion or compromise. "Didn't I tell you devilish thieves you'd die?" he demanded. "Where's Hatch? Where's Sanop? Where's Tuvagutts? And Bob? And Neepooch Grasshopper? Where's Navaho Frank? Now don't you go crying around here for any thousand dollars. Dead men don't need any money."

The old man walked on as if glad to waste no more time on such trivialities. He had dismissed the matter as if his words were final— no possibility of their failure— and it made no difference at all what Mike thought about it.

As to Mike, his wide mouth fell slowly ajar. He gazed absently after Haskel. He thrust his hands in his pockets and drew them out again, still watching the old graybeard disappear down the street.

Mike made no further mention of indemnity, great or small. He and his squaw tied their chattels on their saddles and departed in silence for Navaho Mountain. There they resolved to stay, beyond the zone-limit of Haskel's deadly medicine, in hopes of dodging the fate that had befallen Hatch and Sanop and the others.

CHAPTER TWELVE

DUCKI

Posey's loftiest ideal of dash and power was a horse—a creature able to pass all competition and disappear as a doubtful speck on the far-away hill. He visualized a brute which would strike fire from the rocks with its steel-shod hoofs and slip like an arrow into the blue distance. He knew the barbarous secret of extracting from a cayuse every calorie of strength tucked away under its yellow hide.

The super-gun, the dagger-like knife, the invincible mustang—it was these terms that had worn deep ruts in Posey's mind since his childhood at Navaho Mountain. Yet there was a higher glory than having the best horses: that was to have got that horse by stealth or cunning—to have stolen it or, even better, to have won it by the flip of a card. There was higher glory still: to have won it at *ducki* from a bitterly proud enemy. For this very reason, since Bitseel guarded his horses night and day, Posey pined all the more to meet him with his cards on the blanket.

These smoldering enemies would not speak when they met, but would stalk past each other in contempt pretending not to see. Yet, when a game of *ducki* attracted them like flies to a bowl of molasses, they had a way of eliminating all other flies from the bowl and carrying on to the finish in a battle too exclusive for any third player to share.

The game held them in the devil's grip. They raised their bets to a malicious figure, regarding gains or losses as blows delivered or received. When

Bitseel won Posey's horse and saddle, and the promise of three more horses, and on top of that the promise of still a fourth horse, something in Posey's thinking apparatus exploded. "You thieving coyote!" he raged. "My pinto stallion that you stole is worth more than all four of these horses!"

He threw the cards in the Navaho's face, kicking the blanket after them.

"My sorrel and stocking-footed are worth three of the stallion!" hissed Bitseel, squaring himself for any emergency.

Like fighting tom cats they lunged at each other, settling their claws in the flesh or the hair with vicious tenacity. Bitseel's superior strength and size could hardly match the Paiute's lungs and endurance. After an hour of blood and dirt and curses, they yielded to exhaustion, their faces and limbs red maps of fury, their clothes hanging in shreds or tromped into the dust.

This terminated a kind of righteous lull in Posey's wickedness. It is barely possible that he might have remembered Haskel's warning and continued half-straight a little while longer except for this ill-timed meeting. The evil things in his nature were stirred up now as an ant-hill with a hoe. He stole everything within his reach. Anything he could take from the big Navaho was doubly choice, even though he spent ten times its worth in getting it and had no use for it when he got it in his hands.

Yet these years with their tempestuous *ducki* and their blood, their disastrous losses and their dishonorable gains, these were the happy years of Posey's bruised and checkered life. From its bitterest moments he found respite in summer when he camped at

Peavine or some other cool spring on Elk Mountain.
There he could hunt and rest and watch his two little
boys playing that they had stolen Bitseel's horses, and
had whipped Bitseel with a hard twist rope when he
followed after them. In the solitudes of the tall timber
with Toorah and the children, Posey enjoyed to the
full whatever his tribulations had earned.

However much he may have loved the old Navaho
Mountain where he was born, he loved the Elk
Mountain more. In its forests and by its crystal springs
he spent long and happy days with Toorah, his
cherished companion in all the turbulent trails he was
wont to follow. From the time when the two of them
hid there in terror of her brother, every day they
spent on that mountain had been wonderful. Posey
cherished Toorah as the better part of the life he fought
so hard, even if so foolishly, to maintain, and they both
cherished the mountain as their valued inheritance.

Their love and the joy of it was the love of which
the poet speaks, which, in memory of past happiness,
becomes the chief ingredient of sorrow.

Whatever act in Posey's distracted life may seem
blameable, no one may challenge his devotion and his
constancy to the sweetheart of his youth, the sweetheart who clung unfalteringly to him from the time
of their first meeting in the wild panic at La Sal.

Since early in their married life the blissful spell
of an enchanted honeymoon rested on every place which
afforded them shelter. Then came a proposal by the
government to move all the Paiutes out of San Juan
County, Utah, and settle them on a reservation in
Colorado. San Juan had never been designated as
their country; they had occupied it contrary to orders.
However, it was the land they had inherited from their

fathers, and from their fathers' fathers. It was a dear part of their thinking and of their way of life.

And now the government again ordered them to leave their San Juan and go to Colorado, where they would have no historic Old Trail over which to retreat when they stirred up excitement. They were ordered to leave their San Juan which they loved as part of their own lives, and to go to a strange place which they did not love at all. They flatly refused to go, maintaining their right to stay in the fatherland.

Would Posey leave San Juan and their dear old mountain? Would he leave the trail where every scene had been sanctified by Toorah's presence in the company? He declared he would never go. Mancos Jim, Poke, Scotty, the tribe in general, and every one of its members in particular, swore they would never move a step. Mancos Jim said his fathers were sleeping in Allan Canyon on the east side of Elk Mountain, his own bones should rest there with them. His protest became the slogan of the tribe. They wouldn't go— they would fight it out to the death in the homeland.

The matter dragged along for some time and then seemed to die out. The Paiutes supposed the proposition had been abandoned. Uncle Sam seemed to have no appetite to follow them over the Old Trail.

Again somebody agitated the question into life. Government officials, some of them in uniform, visited San Juan. They counted the Paiutes, took stock of the situation, and declared the tribe must move.

Again the tribe, individually and collectively, declared they wouldn't go. Their bones should rest with the bones of their people. They would fire their last cartridge and take the Old Trail which had been the sure defense of their fathers. They would not go!

Nothing was said again for a long time. The Indians believed their threats and firmness had moved the government from its purpose. Yet the issue was not dead as they supposed. Once more the threat of transfer became active. Government officials came, advising the Paiutes that Uncle Sam was their friend, but that they would have to do as he said.

The Paiutes made the same uncompromising answer, stating it even more firmly: San Juan was their country; they had inherited it from their fathers; no one had a right to order them out of it. They positively wouldn't go!

They didn't go, neither then nor since. They are there still. The bones of Mancos Jim are resting in Allan canyon with the bones of his fathers.

All the tribe, and Posey in particular, believed they had overawed and intimidated the government. Who had ever punished anyone for the murder of the two men at the monuments or for the massacre of the three men at Paiute Springs? Who had ever punished them for the deaths of the fourteen white men at La Sal? Or for the two at Soldier Crossing? Or for the murder of seventeen other white men at various times, for various reasons? Who had ever taken them to trial for their robbings, great and small? Uncle Sam had never been able to do anything, or at least he was not so inclined. Uncle Sam had found the Paiutes too hard to handle. Why should the Paiutes be afraid?

If this erroneous notion about the government had not been strengthened in Posey's mind by all the chief experiences of his life up to that time, and then by unfortunate confirmations for years thereafter, he might have lived to a ripe old age.

The threatening cloud of exile from home was
removed. The dear Elk Mountain should now be his
lifelong hunting ground, Peavine his summer home.
Better than all else, Toorah was his own in spite of her
grizzly brother Poke and the hostile other three. For
a time Posey's pathway was strewn with roses. These
days were the happiest of his strange life. But the
future hung dark with disaster and sorrow.

CHAPTER THIRTEEN

A DARK PASS

In July 1893, love and peace reigned in the little Paiute camp at Peavine. The camp consisted of the renegade Chee-poots, tottering and white-haired with age; the surviving one of his two squaws; Posey, Too-rah and her two little boys; Scotty and his young wife.

They had venison, buckskin, flour, bacon—everything needful in abundance. They hunted and rested as they pleased, every day a holiday. Their goats with bulging paunches gave milk aplenty. Their sleek ponies carried them over the trails in ease and style. They had Bitseel's invincible sorrel to inspire special chuckles of exultation, and they had in mind a cherished list of attractive horses to take away and exchange for their winter supplies.

In August, according to their lately established custom, they went to spend a week feasting on fruit and melons at Bluff. They camped under a spreading cottonwood on the river bank below town, and drove their horses out on the sand hills to the west. Bitseel came by, and although he wouldn't deign to look at any one of them openly, he secretly scrutinized every animals in their outfit. But, of course they had brought with them no horses which might be replevied.

Into their cool cover of green limbs they brought sacks of peaches and melons, slyly appropriated from town, and relaxed to enjoy these refreshments as a pleasant change from the fruits of the wilderness. Then in a state of well-fed good nature they stretched on the cool earth surrounded by scattered melon rinds and exchanged little pleasantries as the occasion demanded.

Posey liked to put on a sham quarrel with his wife wherein he bantered and pretended to scold her with unreasonable demands. He loved her face and her voice, and she returned his banter in the same vein, always with a keen relish. She was beautiful, that was conceded by all who knew her whether white man or Indian. She was still the girl who loved him and went on loving him in spite of her grizzly-bear brother.

In mock sternness, Posey ordered her to go bring the horses in from the sand hills. He didn't want the horses—she knew that— and she knew he wouldn't ask her to get them even if he did want them.

"Go on, bring in the horses. Bitseel will be driving them off. *Tooish apane!*" Posey ordered again.

Toorah understood perfectly the familiar element of love in his unreasonable order. Pretending to defy him she refused to move from the blanket where she lay at his feet.

"Go on," Posey repeated in tones she had enjoyed in their love-quarrels before. "Go bring in the horses or I'll shoot with this pistol!" He knew that it was empty. Still she refused to move as he flourished it above her. Posey thrust it menacingly towards her in mock anger and pressed the trigger. There was a flash, a sharp explosion! Toorah shrieked and tried to rise.

Posey gasped in horrified disbelief and let out a wail of anguish. Dropping the hateful pistol and grasping his beloved Toorah he sobbed wildly.

The little camp went into a panic of dismay. For ten terrible minutes they scarcely knew what they did or which way to turn. They ran out of their green bower only to turn back moaning and crying. They uttered half-spoken words and thrust their fingers wildly through their black and disheveled hair. Posey, delirious with grief, ran among them howling in despair.

And all the time, the poor Toorah lay moaning in agony on the ground, the great forty-five calibre bullet having torn through her hips from left to right, shattering the entire pelvis.

Emotional exhaustion restored Posey's ability to think. He raced to town and implored Aunt Jody Wood, the Mormon nurse-woman, to came at once. He knew if anyone could save his Toorah, she could. Dropping everything, as she always did at the call of distress, Aunt Jody hurried down through the fields to the river bank. By her seeming magic of faith and skill this resourceful woman had accomplished wonderful things through the years, and the Indians tried to hope she could save Toorah. For thirteen years she had been the only doctor in the remote little village, and little had happened there to baffle her skill.

But this was a hopeless case. Aunt Jody saw at once that it was a fatal wound. In tears and anguish she bent over the stricken wife and mother and cleaned and dressed the terrible wound. There was nothing more to do but express her sympathy and leave them to meet the stern inevitable, for it could not fail to come within a very few days.

Day and night Posey watched over his doomed companion. He neither ate nor slept. He gazed at the dear face distorted with pain. He heard the dear voice in anguish which he was powerless to relieve. The most famous medicine men within reach were brought to sing over Toorah, and the songs went on without intermission. Their voices of pleading and prayer never ceased, no matter how late or early the hour.

When calamity comes to a Paiute camp they take it to mean the evil one is in the place, and they move. The Chee-poots clan moved from the big cottonwood on the river bank to a grove west of town. There, on the third day after the tragedy, they saw the life-light fade from the deep brown eyes. They broke up in haste and confusion and abandoned that place.

It mattered little where the next camp was made. To the grief-stricken Posey it mattered little whether it were made at all. Their ponies, tied to the trees, might wait there under their saddles or under their loads to starve for grass or choke for water. What the difference—Toorah was gone! Her still form lay there on the blanket by the tree, her face still beautiful with the bloom of young womanhood. But the light had gone out of her eyes. Deep gloom hung on the cliffs and over the valley.

No matter how empty the world she had left behind, she must have a good horse to ride in the wondrous hereafter. She must have her own little brown pony on which she had come from Peavine. Also her body must be consumed with fire —no evil thing could defile it or prey upon it.

While Posey, oblivious to everything else, had bent in anguish over his sinking loved one, news of the tragedy reached the outside world. Someone with raised quirt, and possibly with a foolish little hat strapped over his heavy hair, had ridden fast and far to tell Poke that his sister had been murdered.

"*Pu-neeh!*" the old grizzly bear had groaned in anguish of wrath. "This shall be the end of the skunk."

Another rider, more kindly than the first, had traveled at horse-killing speed to give warning that Poke was coming in terrible fury. The time might be too short for Toorah's funeral fire —her brother might come with death in his hand before the service could be completed. No difference, the service must be given whatever the cost.

While the Chee-poots horses waited, tied to the trees sufficiently distant from the death camp to escape its evil spell, Posey and Scotty carried Toorah's body up to a cave by the mouth of Buck Canyon. There they placed her tenderly on a heap of dry brush and limbs. Then they heaped more brush and limbs over her till she could not be seen. All the time they cast apprehensive glances across the valley, lest the old grizzly take them unaware.

As they fired the brush, and the air-current through the cave fanned it quickly into a red roaring inferno, they led the little brown pony up over the big rocks and killed it near the fire.

Posey knew that Poke might appear at any minute. All the same that fire had to be kept burning. Through the long night the brothers watched and replenished the flame, watching, too, for the menace that might attack them from the darkness. The leaping flame was a perilous beacon to every lurking danger.

At midnight the haunting shape persisted in the glowing coals. As morning approached it lingered there in the red heap as if clinging to the dear ties of earth. In the gray dawn came another rider —Toorah's brother was very near. Wild with sorrow and anger, Poke sped onward like a poisoned arrow. His horse reeked with muddy lather. The old grizzly wanted but one look at the renegade's son. He would spare nothing until he found Pu-neeh who killed his little sister.

At last the dear form crumbled in the ashes. Now they could fly—but where? Poke would find them west of Wooden Shoes. His curse would overtake them on the Trail of the Fathers. Wherever they fled, he would be a wolf on their trail—a mad grizzly in their path. He would stalk them to the ends of the earth. Even now he might be waiting to attack them some distance away to avoid defiling this sacred ground. Nothing would appease his wrath but blood for blood. If they escaped him, their stay would be long, possibly they would never return.

In the whole distracted world of their acquaintance, with none of it beckoning them to come, they could think of no more promising region than the old mountain of their nativity. There was no time to deliberate. They would go at once to Navaho Mountain, at least for the present.

Setting each little boy on a pony, Posey told them to ride fast and follow him. Scotty and his squaw brought up the rear. Chee-poots and Scotty's mother were to follow at their leisure when they could steal away unseen.

The fugitives toiled wearily off through the reservation turning their searching gaze to the hills behind. They avoided the open trails wherever it was possible till the night covered them. Then they raced anxiously on through the darkness, frantic to hide in the cherished familiar dens of their childhood before the direction of their flight should be discovered.

The dreadful nightmare of the last five days hung ever before Posey's weary vision. He saw it enacted again and again. The terrible moment of the shot,

Toorah's agonizing shriek, his wild despair and Aunt Jody's confirmation of his deepest fears. His utter helplessness to ease his beloved Toorah's suffering, the hours of anguish as he watched the flickering life-light die mid the din of the medicine men. And finally the dragging hours at the funeral pyre where he awaited Poke's fury in dread suspense.

In the weary afternoon of the second day in flight, the coveted mountain towered before them with sweet promise of rest when, all without warning, they met Tsabekiss face to face.

"Hawde nagaw?" (Where are you going?) the old man asked. His searching appraisal of the fugitives showed that he knew something unusual had brought them there on jaded animals. Posey and Scotty answered him with the most likely lies they could devise on the spur of the moment, but they knew he believed nothing of what they said.

This was a calamity! A bad, bad omen! Whatever Tsabekiss knew, Poke could easily find out. Poke would come to him for information. Then the old man would direct him with keen relish to their hiding place. That is, Poke would come unless they waylaid him somewhere along his trail, but that would mean a long and bloody conflict. They would still have to dispose of his two brothers, and then there would be his son, Tse-ne-gat. They might even have to do that and risk never being forgiven by the tribe. No telling how the trouble would terminate.

Just ahead of the fugitives lay a region of smooth rock. Reaching it, with the hateful old Navaho well out of sight behind them, they turned sharply north from their course, leaving no trace nor track on the hard, naked surface to show where they had gone.

Next day they crossed the San Juan River and late in the evening found their way to Clay Hill Spring.

They knew Clay Hill Spring was no safe place to hide, so with the first dim light of morning, they worked their way with their horses up the high cliff to the south. On the top of the high mesa, they found plenty of green grass and the tracks of mountain sheep. A string of holes in the solid rock-bottom of a little gulch held plenty of water from the recent rains. They stopped to remain there indefinitely. They could guard their tracks up the cliff. If no one came too soon, the rains would obliterate their trail and they would be lost to the rest of the world.

Removed at last from immediate danger, they paused in their lofty solitude to think—to mourn for the dear Toorah. They wailed and howled aloud according to the venerable custom of their ancestors. They cut their long hair straight across below their ears. They cut the hair of the little boys and urged them to wail aloud—being removed from their people they could not employ professional mourners as custom demanded and as the dead deserved, so they must do justice to the occasion as best they could.

Toorah was gone! To Posey it seemed that her going had roused the old enemy which her coming had pacified. From their heights of safety there where men might not go once in many centuries, they kept close watch on their trail leading up the hill. As yet it had not rained—their tracks remained a howling declaration of their hiding place. Often they descended to scan the bottom of the canyon deep below them, venturing down on guarded, trackless feet to make sure no one had passed down the canyon since their coming. Old Chee-poots and Scotty's mother would hunt in vain for them at Navaho Mountain.

CHAPTER FOURTEEN

BUCK GRASSHOPPER

Poke arrived in Bluff in a ferocious mood. Anger and weariness had intensified his fierce, brutish nature. He gazed bitterly at the smouldering embers at Buck Canyon, grunting under his breath the fury he could hardly contain. His consuming desire was to be avenged of the skunk before he lay down to rest.

People who knew about the tragedy tried to explain to Poke how it had happened.

"Why be angry with Posey?" pleaded Henry. "He feels worse than you."

"Pu-neeh!" growled Poke. "Let me see him! Let me get just one look at him!"

"He thought the pistol was empty," urged Henry.

"Has he no eyes? He is a skunk! Let me find him!"

With hostile step Poke went to the Chee-poots wickiup. There he found the two old people sitting sadly alone. "Where is he?" he demanded.

They made no answer.

"Why did he kill my sister? Where is he?" he growled.

"He thought the gun was empty," urged old Chee-poots imploringly. "It was a terrible accident."

"Child's talk! I'll find him!" Poke answered rudely.

* * * * *

Buck Grasshopper followed Poke's trail like a coyote follows a wolf. He kept always just out of sight and ran like a frightened puppy from the bare chance of meeting face to face. Ever since that merciless beating over the pinto pacer, he had nursed his hate and whetted his appetite for revenge. But he hated himself for his lack of an old woman's nerve to hide in the rocks by Poke's trail and settle the account in true Paiute style.

Whenever the old grizzly was in trouble or otherwise occupied, Buck made it a point to prowl nearby for any possible mischief or annoyance he could devise. He darted in and out, always with white-feather precaution against being seen.

Poke, bent on finding Posey's tracks, went for his horses where he had left them to graze for a while. They were gone! Sometime in the few hours since he had left them, they had disappeared. He soon found their tracks leading off down the river. Some one had driven them at a furious gait. It was Posey, of course. Who but the skunk would be so eager to leave him afoot?

Back he went with fierce strides to the bower of old Chee-poots. Abruptly he seized the two ponies which the two old people had begun to load for their trip. No time now to stop on ceremony—they could contribute at least these two horses for their part in the trouble. Slamming his saddle on one of the animals and mounting in haste, he led the other on the lope behind him down the river.

Posey couldn't be far away so, instead of delaying for company or cumbersome provisions, the old grizzly determined to take time by the forelock and return from the job before supper. Then his own notions of retribution could be executed with no one to protest or report.

He held to those tracks with grim resolution till evening shadows hid them from his hawk-like glance. Even then he rode on into the night, guessing the direction he should take. About midnight he decided to rest on his saddle until daylight should again reveal the fugitive's tracks.

With the first streak of light he dashed away, lash and curses. Again the eager hours slipped away without giving him a bite to eat. They brought the night down upon him without a blanket on which to rest his weary limbs. Anger drowned his hunger and dissipated his weariness. He cursed to himself as he waited for the day.

In that desperate race Grasshopper had the advantage from the start. He could choose his course without hindrance. He could ride as fast as his horses were able to go without losing time hunting for tracks. If he had been followed by an instinct less keen than that of a wolf, he could have run away and hidden in the distance. But he could not run and hide from Poke.

Grasshopper also had another tremendous advantage. At least, it would have been an advantage to any Paiute with a grain of grit big enough to interfere with the workings of a watch. He could have hidden behind the rocks and exterminated the man behind him as he came along sniffing the tracks.

That advantage availed Grasshopper nothing. His ruling passion was to run like a scared coyote whenever anyone started after him. Now nothing could check his mad flight while his pursuer kept coming.

Buck started for Navaho Mountain but, on his second day in that direction, he remembered Poke's friend, Tsabekiss, who would be sure to give him away. After thinking it over in a fever of fear, Buck turned to the north side of the river, resolving to hide in the solitudes of Pagahrit.

Poke gained on him every mile. Grasshopper couldn't dodge, he couldn't hide his tracks. He couldn't make any turn to throw the old bear off the scent. No bloodhound ever followed a trail more intently than the infuriated grizzly with the wide hat and vertical black mustache.

And no one could shoot with more deadly aim than Poke. On Black Mesa he had shot a deer through the heart while it was in mid-air between two clumps of brush. Remembering that, Buck glanced over his shoulder with a sense of utter helplessness.

He had counted on his speed and his chances of hiding. He had underestimated the deadly intuitions of the wolf from which he was trying to escape. He could neither fly nor hide. Poke would be merciless with him as a wolf with a rabbit. Buck knew this but he had not the nerve to wait behind the rocks as a real Paiute would have done. Frantic with fear and helplessness like a man in a dream, he knew if he failed to do something at once he would be the rabbit in the wolf's jaws.

In that thirsty shadscale country south of Clay Hill, the trail leads up around a little box canyon where a water-hole can be seen in the bottom a hundred feet below. Buck found his way down there for a drink but he had no way to take his horses down. They had to wait on top. In the bottom he shuddered at thought of Poke's coming along before he could get back up. As he returned in double quick time he got a new idea: Shoving his horses off into the ravine ahead, he contrived with nervous effort to get under cover where he could watch for Poke and see whether he descended to that hole for a drink.

Up around the head of the little gulch rode Poke, a grim old grizzly with a wide hat. His two horses were all a-puff and gleaming with lather. Seeing the water in the hole below, he hauled up, swung out of the saddle and disappeared over the rim. Anger, thirst, and exhaustion had distracted the old bear from his usual vigilance. When he caught sight of that water, something for which he had been hopefully looking for the last ten miles, his first concern was to free himself from encumbrances and get down over the ledge to it. The skunk was still running coyote-like just over the next ridge. All that Poke lacked now, to overtake him, was a drink of water.

When Buck saw Poke disappear towards the water, he rode cautiously over to the lathering horses, intending to shove them onward into the ravine after his own. With his enemy afoot, he would quit the country at the same neck-breaking speed he had been following before. But getting nearer to Poke's horses, he changed his mind. The sight of the old bear's rifle hanging in its scabbard, and his pistol dangling in its holster from the saddle-horn, inspired him to seek more permanent escape. Seizing the murderous weapons with trembling fingers, Buck held exultantly, looking toward the rim where the black hat was soon to appear. Now, at last, he could do the thing he had been wanting courage to do since he began—run! He withdrew to a place a little behind the horses and sat ready in his saddle to blast the old grizzly off the earth as soon as he appeared above the rim.

When the wide hat did appear above the rim, and under it the fierce slits of black eyes with their super-human magnetism, it chilled the blood in the coward's veins. His mouth fell open. He sat motionless with his gun at full cock.

In the few times these two had met face to face in the past the dominating personality of the strong over the weak had never been so overwhelming as now. Buck was hypnotized by it! Bewitched as by all the bad medicine ever known among the Paiutes, he was as helpless as a bird looking into the glassy eyes of a snake.

This complete surprise, enough to scramble any ordinary set of wits, even if they were not already weary to death, jarred the equanimity of the old grizzly just a little bit. For a brief second it shook the invincible daring which had carried him safely through all the difficulty and danger of his tempestuous life from the first hair-brained exploits of his wild papoose-hood to the latest calculated schemes of his fierce adulthood.

The surprise was not only in the tremendous matter of his guns being transferred to the hands of his enemy. Up until now Poke had assumed that it was the skunk who was fleeing from him! The skunk would rather compromise than kill, but this dastard wanted more than anything else to make an end of him! And Poke knew he would in a minute shake off his paralyzing fear. And now Buck was more terrified than ever before. Terror had seized on his flesh like an ague.

Poke discerned this wavering and vacillation of the inborn coward —the drooping jaw, the hesitation, the mortal fear. Smoothing the frayed edges of his composure he eyed Grasshopper in silence. Then without a visible tremor he moved sidewise to his horses, and then without shifting his gaze got into the saddle. He knew the stolen horses must be in the ravine just ahead. He moved off towards them, keeping his gimlet-eyes riveted on that trembling gun-pointer lest there come a fateful lapse in his hypnotic spell. As Poke moved, Buck moved, as if a magnetic cord stretched between them.

When Poke reached the stolen horses and moved ahead, Buck followed. He followed his staring enemy on across the shadscale desert. He held the gun in his shaking hands, hands so shaky he could not lift it for dependable aim— at least not under the withering glare of the old grizzly's penetrating black eyes. Buck was powerless to make the first move toward any violent action as long as Poke held him with unseen talons.

They hurried no more, moving on at a pace and in the manner of a troubled dream. Whether he had captured Poke, or Poke had captured him, Buck was not sure. In spite of the guns in his hands he felt a wild impulse to turn and ride for his life.

* * * * *

From their lofty retreat on Clay Hill Mesa, Posey and his brother kept apprehensive watch on the trail in the canyon below them. When they discovered a string of horses and two horsemen coming down the bottom, fear and excitement broke into their quiet little world. Their own trail up the face of the broken cliff was too apparent to escape the searching kind of eyes which Poke always employed. If he were one of those two horsemen, he would not fail to come right up unless he were stopped at the bottom. There was just one way to stop Poke—the way Poke had stopped seven or eight men permanently.

The taller one of those horsemen wore a wide black hat like Poke always wore, and though he was too far away for them to see it, Posey and Scotty felt sure that under the wide brim was a fearsome black mustache. They planned rapidly. They would secrete themselves at two points in the canyon. If one of those men were the brother-in-law, Poke, they would hold up the outfit in the bottom of the canyon, cutting off any retreat forward or back. If either horseman hesitated to surrender, it must be instant death.

When the taller horseman heard a voice of command from the hillside—a voice out of the silence coming as it were from the dead, he looked up with a start into the face of his despised brother-in-law, but quick as light fixed his eyes again on Buck Grasshopper.

And then the old grizzly, poised always on his wits like a cat on its feet, leaped cat-like from that saddle into the rocks. He was out of sight of that other horseman but in full view of Posey, to whom he raised his hands in eager surrender.

For once he did not say, "*Pu-neeh*," nor make any depreciating reference to the spawn of renegades. Instead he called with pleading, yet with command, "Let me take your gun! I'm asking a friend for a gun!"

Not too much surprised nor put out that his extraordinary request fell on mistrusting ears, he repeated, "Let me take it. I won't hurt you. I'll give it back in a minute."

It was the dashing cavalier imploring the lowly skunk; nothing like it ever before. The devoted hero-worship which had driven the poverty-stricken Sowagerie to crawl on his belly after the mighty brave, impelled him now to listen, to thrill with pride, and to yield to the commanding personality.

Approaching without a pause while he talked, Poke was within arm's length of the gun when he heard

a kind of fitful permission to take it. Snatching it
from the skunk's hands he plunged down the hill. The
startled skunk scrambled just as fast back up the
hill, demanding of himself whether he had gone crazy
to let Poke have his gun or whether Poke's bad
medicine had thrown a bedeviling spell over him.

When Poke vanished cat-like into the rocks, Grasshopper had come to a paralyzed stop. He had raised his
gun and dropped his jaw in stupid apprehension. As
he watched vaguely for some movement, that borrowed
gun roared out from the top of a boulder above him.
Buck dropped in a heap from his saddle with no idea
of what had happened to him nor who did it.

"Here's your gun," Poke called, holding it muzzle-
end as he returned it to Posey who had ventured
down in relief to get the precious weapon again in
his own hands.

Meeting the dread glance of the old grizzly, and
trembling as to the outcome of this situation which
had developed like a whirlwind, Posey's first thought
was for the inevitable accounting. "I didn't mean to
hurt Toorah!" he declared with great feeling as a first
bid for clemency. Poke waved the matter aside for the
time being, and beckoned to where Grasshopper lay
dead on the sand.

As soon as the immediate wherefore of this freak
predicament could be explained, Poke and Posey began
discussing their strained relationship. Posey wanted
to know just what and how much he would have to do
to atone for his mistake before the tribe in general
and before his powerful brother-in-law in particular.
Poke wanted to ascertain how much he could require
and collect from the offender.

Remembering the words of Henry and others, and seeing Posey's deep remorse, Poke had to admit that, however awful the tragedy, it was an accident and nothing more. Yet he determined to exploit every advantage it might offer him, not only for gain, but to strengthen his supremacy.

He had abandoned all thought of a blood indemnity, yet he resolved to force a stiff contract on the renegade's son. Nothing in this affair nor ever in anything else, generated in his soul the least love for his brother-in-law. As to the tenderness of real forgiveness, that was minus in his calendar of capacities.

Item at a time and with cautious use of any word which might set off the tinder in Poke's war-loving soul, they worked out the terms of peace. First, it was understood that Poke would not then nor at any future time consider this a cause for any act of violence or harm to Posey. Posey began to relax. He was to be unmolested, but he was to deliver twenty head of horses to his bereaved brother-in-law.

More than that—very much more! He was to marry another of Poke's sisters. She was an old girl left from the first picking, and she had become a troublesome liability in Poke's inheritance. He was more than willing to part with her.

As to this other sister—if all the beauty-elements in old Norgwinup's clan culminated in Toorah, the youngest, all the opposite elements culminated in Spoorka, the oldest. If Paiute law had forbidden cruel and unusual punishment, Posey felt it would have been unlawful for Judge Poke to insert that marriage clause in his sentence.

Even so, Posey was delighted to have the trouble settled so soon and in terms which looked bearable.

He bowed meekly to all the stipulated conditions, and took the starved and exhausted Poke to his lofty lair for food and rest.

After a few days they came down out of the rocks together, turning their faces towards their old haunts where the indemnity was to be paid and the marriage executed.

The old-maid sister, bartered in this deal like a horse or a blanket, must have found it a very interesting item of information when her grizzly brother broke the news to her that he had not killed Posey as at first intended, but instead had required him to marry her. Whether she was shocked or delighted at her appraised value in the transaction, she yet refrained heroically from asserting her sentiments to the embarrassment of her brother's orders. Before that score of horses could be delivered, she became Posey's new wife.

For Poke the arrangement promised a fitting solution to a long tangle of unpleasantries fomented in his household. Moreover, it accomplished something of great diplomatic importance. It hung around the neck of the turn-coat's son a millstone from which he could not soon get away.

From the day the marriage clause of that reprisal was executed on Posey, a new agency began expanding the evil—and withering the good—in his strange world of adversity.

CHAPTER FIFTEEN

BATTLES IN BLUFF

With the new helpmeet Posey went back to Elk Mountain, but he had no heart to make headquarters at Peavine as before —its groves and trails smote him with memories of the dear Toorah. So he drew off to the south end of the mountain, made camp at a spring on Long Point, and claimed that spur of the mountain for himself and for Scotty and the little boys, Jess and Anson.

No one had a better right than Posey to claim for himself a part of that mountain. If it had been only what such a claim is supposed to imply, it would have met with no objection. But Posey wanted the region for his very own, every mile of it! He expected everybody else to stop short at its outer border. Even this unusual demand might have been tolerated by everyone if it hadn't come to light that Posey was stocking the forbidden area with horses not his own.

His passion for the old game was inflamed afresh by the new order of things. It offered him a kind of escape from his sorrow for Toorah. It gave him temporary relief from the nagging and monotony of her sister. More horses without cost—there was in the game a strange, resistless charm. Even after he had delivered the stipulated twenty to Poke, Posey went on getting other scores of horses with rising appetite.

Inseparable from his passion for horses was his lust for *ducki*, with its unfailing thrill of gain or loss. In this drunken realm of spades and clubs and hearts and wild greed, Posey had a feverish itching to match

wits with his old Navaho enemy, Bitseel. There was
only one game more fascinating; the game of getting
away by stealth with Bitseel's top horses.

Like strong drink to the disconsolate, these things
offered Posey a brief respite from the torture of his
unhappy environment, a few hours of forgetfulness
for Toorah. And a few moments of oblivion from the
millstone hung about his neck in her place.

After one of his bouts with Bitseel, from which
Posey came out the small end of the horn, his brother
Scotty and his son Jess happened to meet the big
Navaho alone in the street at Bluff. They stopped
him and mocked him and tormented him in the middle
of the road. When seven Navahos at the store discovered what was happening to their tribesman, they
ran to his relief, beckoning him to hold the Paiutes
till they came. Bitseel succeeded in holding Scotty,
but Jess broke away and ran over the hill to his father's
camp in the mouth of Cottonwood.

In five minutes Posey appeared on the hill brandishing a butcher knife. He ran with all speed to the
knot of men around his brother, reaching for them
with the knife in terrible gesture. They scattered before him like sheep before a wolf.

This was only one in a long series of turbulent
encounters. Whenever Posey and Bitseel appeared in
the same vicinity, they inevitably met. And their
meetings inevitably triggered an explosion as from
the impact of discordant elements. Sometimes the explosion resulted slowly through a card game, a horse-
trade, or an accusation; sometimes it went off with
a bang at the very first contact.

Once when the old log store at Bluff was crowded
with Indians of both tribes, Posey came elbowing his

way through the jam to the counter. When he unin-
tentionally bumped into the big Navaho with the little
hat strapped down on his head like a chip on his
shoulder, there was a quick snarl, a scuffle; Posey
snatched the little hat from under its throat-latch and
slapped Bitseel with it in the face. Pandemonium broke
loose. They thrashed about like fighting cats, leaping
one at the other. The crowd rushed outside or leaped
the counter to avoid them. Each one settled his fingers
in the other's long hair. There was a terrible ripping
of collars and waist-bands.

When most of their clothing was torn away, including the Navaho's G-string, when their bodies were
streaked with bloody scratches, and when like fighting
roosters they had reached a point where they could
do nothing but pull feathers, the store-man succeeded
by threats and diplomacy to bring about a stay of
hostilities. But neither the store-man nor any one else
was ever to stop the fight permanently while both of
them lived to carry it on.

*   *   *   *   *

To his self-appointed reservation on Long Point,
Posey gathered horses from many quarters. He preferred mares for he had got another valuable *peechoogy*
(stallion) and he planned to raise some fine horses
of his very own. If the animals had but been his to
begin with, he might have developed a good business.
Even so he might have done fairly well if he had been
more discreet in his illegal operations.

A dangerous heresy was vitiating Posey's already-
unorthodox standards. Somehow he got the notion that
he had a unique immunity from punishment and
penalties as they were suffered by other men. He
believed he was immune to the penalties of Uncle
Sam's laws, immune to Haskel's medicine, immune

to Poke, to Bitseel, to every adverse influence except
the incessant nagging of the second wife.

If ever he found immunity from her endless com-
plaints, it was because he developed a shell too tough
for her calloused old bill to penetrate. Every day she
told him in murmuring tones just how her brother
would do the things in which Posey failed. Why didn't
he do it this way? That way? He contemplated her in
despair. Posey thought bitterly of Toorah and happy
days beyond recall.

When Posey first arrived as a tousle-headed papoose from Navaho Mountain, he was informed by the
settlers that Uncle Sam's way was absolute; that
Uncle Sam made the laws and punished lawbreakers.
His later observations convinced him that all this was
empty bluster. How had Uncle Sam punished Mike
for killing the two men at the monuments? How had
Uncle Sam punished the Paiutes for killing thirty or
more men since that time? Had not the Paiutes staged
their robberies and hauled away their plunder without
a punishment?

Three times Uncle Sam had tried to move the tribe
out of San Juan. Three times he had failed. Why
should Posey fear Uncle Sam and his laws? Should
he even take trouble to conceal his lawless deals,
present or future? Haskel had predicted that the
thieving Indians would die.

Some of them had happened to die or get killed,
but Posey himself was still going strong. Haskel's
medicine couldn't catch him. More important still,
Haskel himself was dead. No doubt his medicine died
with him.

Twice Poke had sworn to kill Posey, and although
Posey had twice fallen into the bear's paws, unforeseen

events had conspired to save him. He was still very
much alive. Didn't that justify his belief in his immunity? Also Bitseel had tried to whip him and im-
poverish him at *ducki* yet, so far, the score, according
to Posey's estimates, stood handsomely in his own
favor.

Persuaded by this kind of reasoning that he was
really immune, Posey made bold to bring some of his
stolen horses right into town in plain sight of the men
to whom they belonged. When the owners took them
from him, he threatened and fumed. But since there
was no hay in town on which the animals could be kept,
he knew they would have to go back to the grass on the
hills. Why worry? He would soon retake them. By
the law of replevy according to Posey's reasoning,
the settlers might borrow their horses back for a while,
but it would be for a while only. Posey would make
sure of that! It might cause him a little trouble and
delay, yet he would get them all again.

Because of their peace policy the Mormons
wouldn't dare to arrest him or force him into court.
Even if they did, they would be afraid to pass judgment against him. If ever they tried to take him to
prison, they would be taught a stern lesson by his
tribe. What was more, and Posey figured that all the
Mormons knew it and trembled, if they tried to arrest
a Paiute, there would be a worse slaughter than the
one at La Sal. Yes, siree, Posey was a long, long way
from the reach of the law. Why should he worry about
it for a minute!

In prowling over the country hunting his favorite
prey, he found two mares, a gray and a brown, belonging to certain man in Bluff. He rushed them off
out of sight, but not soon enough to miss being seen
by Bitseel who had come with high expectations of

getting the two animals for himself, since they were
of more than ordinary worth.

Exasperated that his old familiar enemy should
beat him again, Bitseel promptly went to Bluff and
told the owner of the mares what had happened to them
and where they could be found.

Without ceremony or explanation, the owner got
the mares in Posey's camp and took them home. Posey
followed him in a fury of curses and threats. Not
that he wouldn't have a chance to steal them again,
but he feared Bitseel would get them first. He had
scored a brilliant point in taking them almost out of
the big Navaho's hands. Now the Navaho had more
than matched the play by taking the owner of the
animals into the game. If on top of all this, Bitseel
got away with them, as he was planning to do, it would
be a stinging defeat to Posey's careful planning.
Posey was more concerned with outwitting the Navaho
than to steer clear of the feeble law of the peace-
preaching white man.

Seeing that his big fuss availed nothing, and that
the owner of the mares would not so much as look at
him, Posey became reckless in his determination to
make his point. He resolved to make the people of
Bluff take notice of his immunity. He began helping
himself to the fruit in a peach orchard and in a choice
melon patch, defying the protesting owner to do anything about it. Repeating what he had heard in the
cow camps he said, "White man talk all time talk,
Damn Injun—me now talk, Damn white man!"

CHAPTER SIXTEEN

FUGITIVES

It was the year 1903, ten years since Toorah's tragic death. Posey had come to be known familiarly as "Old Posey." The two little boys, Jess and Anson, now lacked little of being men in size. Old Posey had become the chief menace of the country. No law had ever reached him; apparently it never would, and he knew it.

His operations imposed such an unbearable levy on the struggling settlers that they began to wonder if, after all, they would not have to surrender to him eventually and move away. As citizens of the United States, they were bound to respect human rights. Posey wasn't. They had to obey the law and earn their bread by the sweat of their brows. Posey was self-exempt from these obligations. Without limitation or restraint, he had conveniently fattened himself on Bluff like a blood-sucking parasite.

Something drastic would have to happen right away or the lawful element would be compelled to abandon San Juan county, leaving it to become a breeding ground for outlaws, who could boldly strip the four border states of every movable valuable.

Posey had his wickiup on a hill just north of Bluff. It was a "summer residence," a little bower built of leafy cottonwood limbs which matted together as they dried, forming a dome-like room twelve feet in diameter with one doorway. On the low red hills were similiar wickiups around him, the camp of Scotty, Milky-eyed Sanop, Old Fatty, and eight or ten more.

When one day, Posey observed the leading men of
the town talking earnestly together, he retired to the
shade of this bower and watched them with amused
concern for developments.

A lone messenger, afoot and unarmed, went from
town to Posey's wickiup with an invitation from the
deputy sheriff to come down and talk matters over.
"No," Posey bluntly declined. He had nothing to say
to any of them. No wish to hear what they had to say.
He wouldn't move a step. The messenger could return
and tell them that much.

Shortly thereafter Posey saw fourteen men coming
from town. Two of them were on horses, and at least
one of them was carrying a gun. Now what did they
imagine they were going to do? He watched with
interest. That persistent second wife watched too, but
neither one moved while the little posse of fourteen
surrounded their bower. Half a dozen of these determined men entered unbidden through the doorway,
but surely they would not dare to touch Posey, who
had dispersed eight Navahos by brandishing a butcher
knife! He was immune to the big government and all
its little pesky communities, especially this tame little
community, preaching peace because it was afraid to
fight.

"We want you to come down and talk with us,"
announced the leading intruder.

"Me no go," grunted Posey in slow and calm contempt.

"You're going with us to town," declared the
deputy sheriff firmly, and three of his men seized the
Paiute as he started to move.

Sharp commotion followed. Quick and lithe and
wiry, Posey almost slipped like a fish out of their

hands. In the struggle a cartridge was kicked into the fire to go off with a bang and add to the confusion.

Surprised and humiliated in being set upon and captured in his own house, Posey turned all his strength and fury loose to vindicate his claim of immunity. He became a violent threshing machine, kicking, striking, twisting till he crashed backward through the wall of the wickiup. Four men fell through at the same time, alighting all over him in spite of his complicated gyrations. With brawny hands they forced his protesting wrists together and clicked the bright handcuffs around them.

But the lord of the wickiup carried on less than half the defense; nobody had begun to estimate the true potential of that second wife. Recognizing with hawk-like eye the first gesture of violence, she sprang for a gun and had it in both hands before any one could reach her. She hung to it like a dog to a bone, swinging now right, now left, with a suddenness and purpose which threatened to bring the gun into action in spite of the husky men who tried to hold her.

Anyone imagining the little Paiute squaw, short and sawed off, is at all frail and delicate, should know what account that second wife gave of herself before the gun was wrested from her sinewy fingers. Then she too became a threshing machine fighting like a wild cat, tearing with its teeth and ripping with its claws.

Yielding to the fact that his wrists were in irons and himself a prisoner in his own residence, Posey looked with consternation first at the bright wristlets and then at the uncompromising faces of his captors. It was terrible. He simply wilted! His limbs relaxed with a strange weakness and he sank in a forlorn heap. Strong hands lifted him to his feet. He sank down again, hoping perhaps to delay the intent of the law. Men raised him up again and churned him up and down before he made any effort to stand on his feet. Face pale, hands a-tremble, Posey reflected that never since he first saw the light of day in Navaho Mountain, had anyone subjected him to any such indignity.

Posey and that second wife were marched down that hill whether or no. Other Paiutes gathered around in surprise and astonishment. Would they fight? Of course they would! They had sworn never to endure anything like this. They had pictured themselves riding insolently over all restraint. But would they fight right now? They considered Posey's subdued expression, and they noted the intrepid spirit of the men who held him. Somehow this little handful of Mormons, fifty miles from their nearest neighbors and a hundred miles from adequate help, looked much less helpless than they had ever looked before.

For some reason unaccountable to them, the Paiutes found no opening to start any hostile move at this time. They would get more of their people before they made any attempt to rescue Posey. For this purpose they sent riders in haste up the river and towards the mountains.

A group of Navahos viewed these proceedings as something entirely new and startling. Among them was the much-gratified Bitseel with his greasy little hat strapped securely down on his hate-loving head.

Jess Posey rode full whip to alert Mancos Jim and his satellites in Allan Canyon. Milky-eyed Sanop went for Poke and his kinsmen at Alkali. A boy went on a fast horse to Montezuma Canyon for Johnny Benow and the big lodges of Indians there with him.

Poke simply grunted. *"Pu-neeh;* He likes trouble. Let him enjoy it."

Johnny Benow took little interest in Posey's dilemma, but some of his neighbors out of curiosity came to see the trial. Mancos Jim received the word at night after he had retired wearily to rest. He lay tossing on his blanket till morning, contemplating the dread possibilities of what legal restrictions might do to the liberty of his people. At daylight he hit out with all his followers for Bluff. There he broke loose like a big alarm clock in a long, cantankerous speech. His "Heap big talk" made no change whatever, and like a clock he ran down at last with nothing more to say. He stood helplessly watching to see what would happen.

Posey was held under close guard, his wrists in irons for some time. When his belligerent squaw finally folded her hands and withdrew, mumbling venomous curses from a distance, the sheriff gave her lord free use of his hands, watching him a little more closely.

Joining her people the angry squaw fanned the flame of their indignation by telling what her brother would do when he arrived, and urging them to be ready to follow his lead. When she heard that Poke cared nothing about Posey's plight or the effrontery of the law, she took the lead. She set about to heat the situation and stir it up till it boiled over. She visited her lord with long exhortations. She coached others with similiar exhortations for his benefit.

Three days of delay brought something like calmness to Posey. Though still under strain, and haunted by what had transpired, he assured his people that he would be released at the trial. This little spoonful

of Mormons, with no means of defense, would not dare
do anything more than they had already done. Their
actions so far were more bluff than reality.

When the county officials sent word that they
couldn't come and authorize the preliminary hearing
to be conducted in Bluff, the Paiutes proudly assumed
that they had intimidated the Bluff people from undertaking to move Posey out for the trial. By the same
token the Paiutes thought they would keep the white
men from taking him out to prison in case he were not
released.

They watched eagerly for the hearing. It was held
in the school house, the room crowded by people from
both tribes and from the settlement. Bitseel was there,
hoping for the worst. Posey was seated on the front
row of benches before Justice Peter Allan. A damaging
array of evidence was presented against him with no
extenuating circumstances. When the defense and the
prosecution had finished their arguments, the judge
deliberated carefully before giving his decision. Suspense reigned. The school clock ticked loudly on the
wall.

Peter Allan, known and trusted always for the un-
faltering courage of his convictions, announced that
the defendant was bound over to appear in the district
court. He was to be confined in the county jail at
Monticello until the time of the court's next session.
When the nature of the decision was interpreted to
the Paiutes a sigh of surprised disappointment ran
through the room, followed by sounds of anger, sorrow, fear, and a rush for the door.

In quick confusion all life disappeared from the
red hills. Posey sat disconsolate in the hands of his
guard, more upset by the decision of the court than
he had been by the arrest.

With all the faults of that second wife, she had not forsaken her man—not yet. Though his camp-neighbors of the red hills thought it wise to withdraw from the fuss, she continued undaunted. With Scotty and her two boys, and Old Chee-poots, she plotted in their camp hidden by thick willows near the river.

As a last resort they would waylay any movement towards Monticello. But they had a better plan to try first. Scotty came to talk it over and get his brother syncronized with all the details of their plan. The people of the settlement anticipated trouble in trying to move their prisoner and planned carefully. The delay necessary in making ready for the hazardous undertaking fitted nicely into Scotty's plans.

When Scotty disappeared again towards the hidden camp, he left his brother and the guard mopping their faces and fanning themselves in the August heat. It looked like the most natural thing in the world for Posey to ask to be allowed to take a cooling dip in the river. Surely there could be no objection to that in this killing heat.

The guard agreed. Walton's Slue being the nearest arm of the San Juan, they went to its willow-grown bank. When Posey had disrobed he plunged into the cool stream. The guard sat meditatively on a log holding a six- shooter ready for action. He watched Posey frisk around in the water, diving and swimming and seeming to enjoy himself. Then suddenly from his floundering around in the water, Posey sank from sight and the stream rippled over him. Where had he gone? Could it be that he had drowned? Not Posey!

His sinking was with malice aforethought. Holding to the sandy bottom of the slue, he propelled himself along down the current with every ounce of his throbbing anxiety. When he had to breathe he raised his nose for a second above the surface and dived frog-like again for dear life.

In great alarm his guard dodged through the thick willows along the bank. He saw his prisoner rise in shallow water and run with great splash for the opposite side. Straining all his nerves to run through water above his knees, Posey heard the sharp roar of the guard's pistol as a bullet whistled past his ears. Defenseless, naked, and panting for life, he stumbled. Again the roar, and still again, while the hot lead sung frightfully near to his bare flesh as he staggered from sight among the willows on the south bank.

Fate decreed that those bullets should miss Posey, that he should have yet twenty years in which to make more trouble in San Juan and raise more hell than he had ever raised before—twenty years and five months. Fate decreed too that these foolish escapades should make Posey, in fifty years, the most famous ancestor of his tribe.

Scotty, hidden among the willows on the south bank of the slue, had been waiting with saddled horses, waiting and watching long before the bathing began. Panting and throbbing from his great exertions, Posey leaped to the back of one of the horses. Together the two brothers raced for the main stream. Through it they rode ker-splash and away into the reservation, a little cloud of dust rising from the sand behind them.

They found the rest of their clan all mounted and ready to go. Posey lost little time diving into clothes which the second wife held ready. Risking no further delay the little group loped away through the hills to the southwest. With eager hopes they set their faces towards Navaho Mountain, keeping a sharp lookout behind.

A posse from town crossed the river in pursuit, but the posse had wisdom to turn back before getting within rifle-range of the rocks.

Beyond the rugged horizon, ahead of the fugitives, rose the dear defense which had sheltered them before. Behind them waited the aroused Mormons, and scattered in the hills were the white-feather Paiutes who had flunked at the critical moment. A storm of rage and fear roared through Posey's senses. Weary months were to drag by before he could know how much this new experience had jarred the base of his composure.

On top of this nerve-racking ordeal, Bluff still visible in the distance, the fugitives met the exulting Bitseel riding one of the mares over which the trouble started. He had that pusillanimous little hat strapped over his Absalom-head-of-hair, and a victory grin on his weather-seasoned face. His custom was never to speak to the Chee people when he saw them, but now he was friendly enough to call out and tell them that he had at his hogan the other mare over which all their trouble had originated.

The Chee clan rode wearily forward all that night. When they finally did think it safe to stop, Posey could not compose himself for a wink of sleep. The next night was the same sleepless torture. So the next night and the next, even though Posey rose in torment five times and moved his bed to get away from the devils hovering over him.

At the native mountain, conditions improved but little. If he dozed it was to start up in terror with visions of handcuffs being thrust on his wrists or of some one firing at him while he tried to run through deep water. Sometimes old Tsabekiss really came prowling around like a spy, compelling Posey to double his vigilance against his enemies, real and imaginary.

Posey dejectedly reviewed his unhappy plight. Uncle Sam had proved to be innocuous — hardly a power to be feared. But that little group of peace-preaching Mormons had suddenly come alive. After pleading for twenty-odd years for peace and seeming to have no fight in them, they had all at once become the boldest men in the world. They had taken him like an unruly papoose from his own wickiup and set him down in irons before their judge. They had pronounced against him without compromise. They had shot at him three times as he struggled in nakedness to get away through the water. The more he reviewed it, the more it distressed him.

More still, they had it written now in their be-deviling books that he must appear before a still-more powerful judge. They would be in eager readiness if ever he tried to go back. Something in their method of law-enforcement whipped him as he had never been whipped before.

In the ever-present apparition of that dreadful power which could come in and carry him from his house and punish him like a bad boy, Posey saw the black piercing eyes of the dead Haskel fixed on him. He heard the gray, bearded lips declaring again, "If you steal our horses or our cattle, you'll die like a dog the same as these other thieves."

Across the San Juan to the north of their native mountain, the Chee-poots clan gazed at the rocks around the Pagahrit. The cattle there belonged to the man who had made trouble about the gray and the brown mares. Those mares were Bitseel's possession but for stealing them Posey and his people were fugitives and outcasts. The owner of these cattle at Pagahrit had appeared against them in court, had argued against them, and was most to blame for their misfortune.

Confined in their native mountain the Chee-poots people felt they were in a sort of prison: nothing to do, little to eat, no one to plunder. If they had something to relieve the monotony, if they could eat their fill, and if they had some one to rob, especially an enemy, Posey might revert to health and normalcy. They decided they could find all they needed to make them happy if they went over to the Pagahrit where their enemy kept his fat cattle.

In a surprising short time they were camped at the old Pagahrit where they had gone with the tribe years before to hold high carnival after the killing at Soldier Crossing. They lost no time in shooting some of the cattle as they had done before. Eating the beef of their enemy and seeing some of his valuable cattle rotting on the sand seemed to be the kind of good medicine which they had been needing. Posey sent word to the owner of the cattle that if he came to get them, he would be left to rot with them on the hills, a feast for the crows and coyotes.

The owner of the cattle punished them in a way of which they had never dreamed. Coming with his men he rounded up the whole Pagahrit region. Taking everything which had survived their vandalism, he drove the stock away over Clay Hill and out of the country. While he and his men rode there, the angry fugitives led by Posey planted ambuscades and waited with murderous intent, gripping their guns and peering eagerly out over the rocks. The cowboys rode within easy range, among them the man responsible for their humiliation, but somehow the hearts of these plotters failed them. They couldn't shoot! They found themselves as badly hoodooed as Buck Grasshopper had been. It gave them a terrible start. The dead Haskel seemed to interpose wherever they lay in wait, his black eyes staring them out of countenance. In astonishment and alarm they peeped from their cover to see the last herd disappear in the distance, leaving them to hold the entire empty country alone.

Little remained for them to live on. No one came. The silent campgrounds and the vacant corrals of the Mormons became dismal to contemplate. The desolate desert rocks of Pagahrit became more oppressive than Navaho Mountain had been. Devils gathered thick around Posey in exile. Legions of hateful demons hovered over his rest at night. Yellow lizards cocked hateful eyes at him over heated rock in the daytime. Owls groaned their maledictions in the darkness. Winds moaning over the weary desert carried voices of strange tormentors who followed him wherever he want. Sometimes he heard again the piercing shriek of the dear Toorah mingled with the echo of that fateful shot. Sometimes in the clouds he saw her sad, sweet face, a vision from which he turned to behold with aversion the hard, dull face of that second wife.

Not all of the Chee-poots people followed Posey through his year and a half of exile, but he was never once relieved of that millstone which Poke had hung about his neck. She stayed faithfully near. Credit may be due her constancy, but she made Posey's world hardly bearable with her incessant nagging. Posey became eager to go back to Bluff and to the Elk Mountain—he was ready to crawl all the way on his hands and knees—if he could just have legal permission to go with immunity from arrest.

He sent a messenger entreating the owner of the mares to withdraw his complaint, and begging the people of Bluff to forgive him and let him come back.

If he could just be free again, he would never make any more trouble! The messenger declared that Posey would soon die if he had to stay in hiding any longer.

Not one voice was raised against his proposed return. The legal charges were withdrawn. He was invited to come as soon as he would. Everybody connected with the arrest and the trial approved the offer of forgiveness, hoping Posey would go straight and emulate the example of Henry.

Posey came at once. He shook hands with everybody in town. He went from house to house, delighted to see his old friends again. He seated himself in the old log store, as happy and as free as a man released from prison. He seemed all at once to love everybody. Everybody held good wishes for him, trusting and hoping he had seen the folly of his ways.

The word, *everybody*, as used here, refers to the people of Bluff only, for while Posey sat there in the store, a stalwart Navaho with a greasy little hat strapped on his head, stopped in the doorway. Raising his eyebrows in amused surprise he exclaimed, *"Aye Law! Pu-neeh!"* which amounts about to, "Well, I declare! The skunk has come back!"

This uncalled-for comment, buzzing as an ugly black fly right into the special ointment of Posey's keen susceptibilities, revived his memory of where he had last seen Bitseel —riding one of the stolen mares and boasting of having the other one at his hogan. Somehow, Bitseel's taunt had a strong tendency to sour the sweetened ointment of the skunk's good intentions, aggravating the old offensive inclinations of his more fallible self.

CHAPTER SEVENTEEN

WHITE MAN'S MAGIC

Posey did not prolong the glad moment of hand-shaking and embracing old friends. Instead he gravitated to the range and looked for a remnant of his former possessions. He had the same ubiquitous second wife at his elbow telling him always how her great brother would do this or that, and how he was ever in disfavor with her brother because he failed to do it that way.

Posey's release from exile had the magic effect of restoring his former health and composure—why should he not pursue the ways of his former life? He was simply Old Posey again, reacting in the very same way to the very same urges of existence. Naturally he began to do the very same things he had done before.

Range-cattle had grazed freely on his Long-Point reservation during his absence. His collection of horses had been for the most part reclaimed by their rightful owners, or had wandered from the point, so he had before him the alluring task of rebuilding his old estate by collecting and adding to his wasted herd. But his strange experience of the last year and a half came with unpleasant echoes back into his mind. The more he recalled it, the more strange it seemed. He felt a necessity to dispose of it, to account for it, or to devise some explanation for it before he could dip freely again into the beckoning game.

His prevailing sense of joy that the strange malady was over, turned into a sense of wonder that it had ever happened—that it could ever have happened. Soon Posey grew to resent and rebel at the very memory of it. He resolved by all the Paiute gods of war that it would never happen again! He reasoned that if he had been properly armed he could never have been arrested. And even if he had been arrested and driven into exile, with a long-range gun he could have returned to Long Point or wherever he wanted to go in defiance of the ordinary saddle-guns carried by the cowmen.

He decided he had been foolish to submit, and more foolish to stay so long in hiding. Henceforth he would be wise. He would be prepared always for trouble. The awful indignity of being seized in his own wickiup and tried in court by white men should never happen again!

After enquiring of the trappers and sheepherders about a long-range gun, he was told he could buy one in Dolores, Colorado. Immediately he began saving his money. Before long he made a special trip and came back with the coveted weapon so deadly at long range. What a marvel! What a winner! He showed it proudly to the other Paiutes and even to the crack-shot, Poke.

From the Paiute point of view, the white man's most worthwhile invention was the gun. The sight of Posey's big rifle whetted the appetite of all his friends to possess one just like it, and some of them had the price. With a thing like that they could stand right out in the open and defy the forty-four calibre man with impunity.

At first Posey tried to keep his defense program a secret from the settlers. When they learned of it, he made bold to warn them in war-like language just what would happen, if ever they tried to arrest him again.

Reflecting less now on the strangeness of his exile Posey forgot how he used to see Haskel's bearded face in the mist. He forgot the devil-legions that used to hover over his bed. He forgot the yellow lizards and the warning wailings of the wind. He began to be consumed with bitterness in his reflections.

He remembered how the deputy sheriff had shot at him and missed him three times even though he was not far away and was laboring slowly through shallow water. Wasn't that proof that he was still immune as he had begun to discover before? He was immune to everything including the Mormons and their dead Haskel. He was even immune to all the unseen or fortuitous agencies which had punished some of his people for taking a few horses or eating a little stolen beef.

Posey bolstered his notion of immunity by remembering a multitude of trivial circumstances where he came out unhurt from what could have been disaster. Along with this he nursed every old grudge and began incubating a whole batch of new ones.

He devised what he called fences around little meadows below springs where cattle went to drink, calling the enclosed land his farm. When range cattle went through these flimsy barriers, as he knew they would, he insisted that the owners of the cattle pay damages. It was a profitable racket, but it was also a big bid for trouble. Posey wanted trouble. The settlers paid many of his claims to prevent, or at least delay, the day of trouble which was impending.

*　*　*　*　*

Not long after Posey's return from exile, the first T-model Ford car came sputtering into San Juan. Roads began to be made more passable. On White Mesa, only fourteen miles from the Paiute homes in Allan Canyon, the Mormons began building a new town to be known as Blanding. Along the improved road from Blanding to Bluff twenty-five miles away, a strange wire was stretched overhead between posts set in the ground. It was reported that by some kind of magic medicine the people of the two towns could talk with each other through that wire.

It looked bad. Then the menacing wire was extended on down the river to Mexican Hat. Posey feared that such incomprehensible devices as this might enable the white men again to carry him bodily from his wickiup. They also had an infernal little machine with a mysterious little round eye on one side. It could open this eye and preserve an exact picture of whatever it saw. What could that be for but to bewitch him and his people? Those settlers had suspicious devices of all kinds. They kept one man busy every day bringing in great leather sacks full of "paper talk," incomprehensible stuff which could bode nothing good.

Posey resolved to investigate some of these things, especially that overhead wire piercing his safety-zone to Mexican Hat. What was to hinder the white men from stretching it on down, possibly right into Navaho Mountain? It might extend into every one of his hiding places and have him more completely hoodooed than when he hid out a year and a half in exile.

Posey went to the phone office in Blanding and asked to send a message to another Paiute in Bluff. He had his positive doubts about the genuineness of the thing. The operator might talk and pretend to receive an answer, but he could ride to Bluff and check whether any such answer had been sent. But he would not touch the thing himself! He would keep at a safe distance.

The operator really did talk into one part of the thing, and seemed to hear something from another part. It really looked convincing. Posey framed his message in pidgin English, but it failed to convey the intended idea from one Paiute mind to the other. So the operator asked the two Indians to do their own talking. Posey hesitated. That white-man contraption might bedevil him with afflictions from which he might never recover.

When the telephone girl induced him to take the thing in his hand, he held it warily at arm's length. If at that minute a short-circuit had given him a shock, he would have leaped with a yell for his cayuse and bolted with his big gun for Navaho Mountain. However, nothing happened to stampede him. He was directed to put the receiver to his ear and the transmitter to his lips. Timidly, and with great hesitation he spoke. In amazement he recognized the voice of his friend in Bluff, but they made no better progress than before. They were still talking pidgin English. The operator wondered why and told Posey to speak in his own language.

What? could this white-man's *awa-pay-ane* (contraption) comprehend Paiute? What dangerous possibilities! It startled him. With fear and uncertainty he ventured a native grunt. Another grunt came in answer and nobody hurt! Posey spoke again. Then he took a more trustful grip on the thing and talked freely.

*   *   *   *   *

After Blanding came into being, Posey made fewer trips to Bluff. Yet he still met the big Navaho with

enough frequency and with enough violence to keep
the old feud crackling vigorously. With Bitseel he
exchanged damnifying words and bloody scratches
at a big *yabetchi* (a great Navaho festival). There
the Navaho discovered Posey's bias for the super-gun,
and he got one for himself so they could meet on equal
terms. Another rival began to steal Posey's fame,
though he didn't arouse Posey's jealousy in the least.
In the years following the glorious exploits at Soldier
Crossing, when the tribe made the grand victory march
over the Trail of the Fathers, Poke began raising a son
after his own heart. This son grew up with ambition
to do not only what his father had done, but to shed
more blood and raise more fury than his father ever
thought of.

This was Tse-ne-gat, more commonly known as
Poke's boy. At nineteen he was the star of first magni-
tude in the Paiute galaxy of thieves, robbers and
murderers. Compared with him, Bitseel and Posey
were tame squaws, and the rest of the plundering
Paiute gang were innocent papooses deserving special
treats for good behavior.

As a desperado unhampered by heart or conscience,
Tse-ne-gat was the prize achievement of his grizzly-
bear father. With a very different child-psychology
from that employed by Chee-poots, Poke trained his
son carefully up in all the ways he should not go. In
his very early adolescence Tse-ne-gat, Poke's boy, was
a firebrand without precedent.

With great frequency from the time of his tender
papoosehood, he listened to his father relate the raid
on the Horse Ranch, the plunder they carried away,
the blood and ashes they left behind. Whenever the old
bear began with it, the boy had to have a repetition
of the whole picture, including the fourteen men laid

out for the crows to eat at La Sal. The boy heard with
glee about the fight at South Montezuma, and relished
the account about the two men dogged to death at
Soldier Crossing. He reveled in the stirring tales of a
long string of occasions where Paiutes had been
glorified with white man's blood. To the eager Tse-
ne-gat, these vivid histories were more than the stories
of George Washington to the wide-awake American
boy.

When Poke's boy was old enough to begin doing
things along criminal lines, his father helped him hold
up a man at gunpoint in the street of the new little
town, Blanding. They compelled the man to pasture
the boy's horse on a field of young wheat. Horse-feed
being very scarce at the time, the boy considered he
had done a very smart trick. Tse-ne-gat grew more
brazen and insolent, more pitiless and cunning, grad-
uating at last with high honors, under his father's
careful tutelage.

Some of the people of his tribe declared that Tse-
ne-gat beat his young wife to death with a hardtwist
rope, and disposed of her body in true Jack-the-ripper-
style. All the contempt of all his people for the laws
of the United States and for the rights of man, was
focused with a vengeance in Poke's boy. But he inherited nothing of the bravery of his grizzly-bear
father— he was yellow to the bone.

CHAPTER EIGHTEEN

THE GRAND EXCURSION

Tse-ne-gat was charged with murdering and robbing a young Mexican sheepherder, Juan Chacon. According to reports, young Chacon had drawn his wages, preparatory to going home on a visit to his wife and child. Poke's boy tried to inveigle him into a game of *ducki*. But Chacon had worked hard for his money, and he was no gambler. He was eager to go with his earnings to the little home he had planned to improve, in the little village of his childhood a hundred and fifty miles away in New Mexico.

Refusing to play *ducki*, he started with his two horses from the mouth of Yellow Jacket to cross the wild country south of McElmo Canyon. It is related— and there is strong proof—that Tse-ne-gat followed him, shot him in the back, and returned with Chacon's outfit and money. Those who knew Poke's boy, and heard the evidence against him, gave him full credit for the murder.

Officers from outside the county arrived with warrants for the boy's arrest. But whatever the efficiency of those officers in the area where they had been accustomed to operate, they failed miserably in San Juan. So poorly were their plans framed and executed, that the whole Paiute tribe lacked little of being on the warpath before any substantial steps had been taken toward Tse-ne-gat.

Grizzly old Poke refused to recognize the right of the government—or of anyone else—to call his tailor-made son to account. With his big gun and his crack

markmanship he resolved to defend his boy at all costs.
To accomplish this end he wielded with his people the
tremendous influence which he would not use for
personal glory or promotion. His instinctive supremacy, his cool nerve, his splendid action and accuracy
with a gun, his utter disregard of praise or blame, and
his tenacity of purpose, made Poke the chief of his
tribe whenever he wanted to shoulder the responsibility of that rank. The entire tribe, with a few ex-
ceptions like Henry, stood eager to do his bidding.
Even Posey, despised as a skunk, wanted to crawl on
his belly and fight the old bear's battles, if only his
grizzly-old-highness would accept his service.

Poke, however, with his lifelong prejudices against
the renegades, wanted none of their spawn among
his immediate circle. Posey therefore, camping as near
as he dared to the big cavalier, had his camp two miles
down the river at Sand Island. Poke and his cabinet
had their group of wickiups just west of the mouth
of Cottonwood, half a mile northwest of Bluff. Poke's
suspicions had been aroused by the ill-advised actions
of the officers from the outside. He preferred this
place near Bluff as the most suitable vantage from
which to spy on everything that went on.

A posse of fourteen men camped off the road
out of sight at Three Cedars, fifteen miles north of
Bluff. It was the intention of these men to come in the
night to surprise and capture the camp where Poke
was sheltering his boy.

Surprise and capture the old grizzly? How little
those officers from far away knew what they were
talking about! Poke's knowledge of war in the rocks
was instinctive. His instinct for self-preservation and
cunning were as accurate and as deadly as that which

nature has given to the animals to protect them from the plots of men.

True, Poke could not comprehend the printed page. His schooling had been with nature, not with art. But if that little squad of plotting officers had known how many keen eyes Poke had for seeing, how many keen ears he had for hearing, and how sharp were his intuitions for grasping the meaning of cryptic actions and words around him, they would have been fearful of his surprising and capturing them. Actually, in the impending fight Poke lacked little of doing that very thing. At midnight the men at Three Cedars mounted their horses and headed toward the Paiute camp hoping to find the old bear and his people fast asleep. It was a cold raw night in February 1915. When they reached Bluff they had to thaw out before they were limber enough for action. Surely on such a night the Indians would be huddled under their blankets, secure from the frost and winter outside. Surely— wishful thinking!

With the utmost care to make no noise the posse rode out to surround the camps. It was still dark, though a doubtful glow had come in the eastern sky. The wickiups, winter residences made of logs and heaped over with earth, looked like so many shapeless mounds in the gloom. Everything seemed quiet as the horsemen reached the first position from which they intended to call for surrender.

Then something moved in the dark camp—something stealthy and feline. A blood-curdling yell rent the air. While that yell still echoed in the cliffs, north and south, another yell pierced the cold night air. It was the roar of the grizzly chief summoning every member of his cabinet to come with his gun.

Bright flashes broke sharply into the darkness
—flashes from the camp and from the posse. Chicken
Jack fell before he could reach cover. A squaw dropped
with a mortal wound. Havane and a dozen other
Paiutes had to surrender, but most of the people of the
wickiups dropped into a little sandwash or fled to the
tall greasewoods. There from their cover they threatened the safety of the posse still out in the open. They
forced part of the posse into a little cove of the cliff
where they had to climb ignominiously to the top for
their lives, leaving their horses behind.

Whenever a white man moved, bullets whistled
through the brush or plowed into the dust. All hands
sank from sight and lay low in suspense. Over this
game of waiting, came the slowly increasing light
of day, showing clearly where they had blundered
around in the darkness and failed to go where they
should have gone.

The main part of the posse had no idea what had
become of that part of their numbers forced into that
cove beyond Cottonwood. They took Havane and the
other prisoners to a little hall over the co-op store in
Bluff, but they could only guess where the rest of the
Indians had gone and where trouble might next spring
out.

Poke with his wide hat had been seen to disappear
in a sandwash among the greasewoods. He was supposed to be peering from its shelter for someone at
whom to shoot. Joe Aikin, one of the men of the posse,
lay flat on the ground with only one eye visible above
the hill. He was looking for the old bear to peep from
his sandwash. James Decker, a Bluff man, stood full
length on the top of the hill watching both sides of the
fight. The dead Haskel still dominated Poke as he lay
there under cover so, instead of shooting at Decker,

an easy mark, he sent a bullet through Aikin's head above that one visible eye.

Somebody reported the fight to Posey in his camp at Sand Island. Two Indians had been killed. Poke had got one white man and had gained a commanding position on the cliffs. *Pu-neeh* grabbed his gun and straddled his pony. Poke had added to his glory still another white man—how discouraging to be so much outdone! Never so much as one white man to his own credit, Posey lamented, in all their glorious wars.

He raced through the greasewoods towards Bluff. He saw two horsemen. He heard shooting. Everything seemed to be in commotion. What chance did he have to make a good shot from that open flat? He had his long gun, but even then someone might get him before he had a chance to use it.

He saw two horsemen riding rapidly towards town. Apparently they had seen him and resolved to keep out of range. Posey broke off a long stalk from a greasewood. Tying a white rag on the end of it he waved it aloft. When the two men saw the flag of peace they assumed he was a harmless neutral and made no effort to get out of his way as he rode rapidly towards them.

Posey was still too distant for a sure shot when the men approached the bank of the wash where they would disappear from sight. Dropping on the ground among the brush he fired at one and then at the other with his longe-range gun. They sank from sight over the bank. Some one returned his fire from near town, but it was a lowpower gun and the bullets fell harmlessly short.

The men of the posse looked through their binoculars to see who had played the white-flag treason

against them. They saw Posey. He was stooped rear-
ward towards them in contempt as a mock target, patting the seat of his breeches towards them in exultant
insult. One of his bullets had struck Jose Cordova, a
man of the posse, passing between the heart and the
back bone, inflicting a wound which was at once pronounced fatal, but from which Cordova recovered after
a long and painful struggle for his life.

Following this brave act of devotion to Lord Poke,
Posey got around on the cliff to the telephone wire.
He knew just what to do. Triumphantly he cut Bluff
off from all communication with the outside world.
The town was alone and in a state of siege.

Poke and his followers with their long-range guns
held to their vantage postions on top of the cliff overlooking the town. The officers and men moving
cautiously below with ordinary rifles could do nothing.
Not only was it impossible to telephone, but all of
Bluff knew that no man from there could get out
through the narrow pass in Cow Canyon to report
their predicament. Any move to capture the Indians
was unthinkable; the Indians had all but captured
them.

The men of the posse guarded Havane and the
other prisoners in that little hall over the co-op store.
When Havane made a move which one of them said
was a start for a window, they shot him through the
bowels. After suffering several hours he died. No
such thing as keeping this foolish act a secret, and it
vexed the situation all the more.

The Paiutes, seated there on top of the world with
their big artillery, lacked little of having full sway
over the men who came against them, and they watched
eagerly for a chance to complete their supremacy.

The posse had barely cared for its dead and its wounded and begun to scratch its head for ideas of how to prosecute the war further, when the Indian Agent from the Ute Reservation in Colorado arrived and ordered the whole procedure to stop—as if it had not already come to an ignominious standstill! He announced that no one but himself had jurisdiction over the San Juan Paiutes. The delay over this ridiculous disagreement was taken by the men on the cliffs to mean they had the posse pretty well hoodooed.

Meanwhile, on the outside, with the wire dead and no messages coming from the southern town, Monticello and Blanding became alarmed. Quickly they raised a force of fifty men who rode down over the frosty road towards Bluff in the night-time. The clatter of all these hoofs on the hard road could be heard in the wilderness for miles. Poke's snipers in their victory nests detected the roar as the cavalcade approached. Without any way of knowing whether it was a hundred or a thousand men, they thought best to get themselves away into some of their defenses until they could see who was after them.

Of course they expected to be followed. That would have been their delight. Then they could live again the glory of the Old Trail, sing the song of Soldier Crossing, and be the united tribe they had been thirty years before. But Oh! how uninteresting these white men were, for no one followed them, although they watched and waited. It was the same dull enemy for which they had waited before.

Somebody in the newest posse did make bold, when all the Indians were out of sight, to burn the substantial wickiups in which Poke's people had lived all winter. They did generously spare one hard-earned hut in which they found a squaw, old and blind, who had been deserted because she could not follow her people to their lookout site.

The Indians regarded that burning as a yellow confession of weakness on the part of the posse. To say the least, it was no act of bravery. It appeared to the Indians that Uncle Sam was unable to cope with the problems they had presented.

All the same be it said of the band of those fifty men, that they arrived in Bluff "rearing to go." They would have left without delay, leaving the Utah officer and the Colorado agent to settle their quarrel for supremacy, but a telegram came from Washington, D.C. ordering everything to stop. The agent lost his coveted glory of being the "big shot" in this Paiute war, and the Utah officers fared no better: General Hugh L. Scott was on his way from the nation's capital to supercede both of them.

More delay—delay which the Indians interpreted to their own glory. The new army of untold numbers, which had sounded like an avalanche, had apparently got cold feet. There was no need for the Paiutes to flee. So they stopped at Douglas Mesa hoping that the trouble had not blown over in so short a time. They craved excitement.

Then the word was taken to them that one of the nation's top chiefs was coming all the way from Washington to see them—coming because they were such difficult men to handle. The general coming to fight them—he had with him no weapons and no men. He was coming to entreat them. This news inspired nothing of fear in the Paiutes—only increased self-conceit in their opinion of themselves as invincibles.

When the general, likeable and diplomatic, approached their hideout on Douglas Mesa, they yielded to his persuasions and surrendered. What was there to fear? The general assured them they would have a fair trial. They took this term to mean, as they afterwards expressed themselves, that no harm or punishment would come to them in going out to the white man's court.

Poke was wanted for resisting arrest and killing an officer. Posey was wanted for treacherous use of the white flag and for his all-but-successful attempt to kill another officer. The white-livered Tse-ne-gat, who had kept safely out of all danger during the fight, was wanted for robbery and murder. Besides these three, the general decided to take Jess Posey along on general principles, or because, being Posey's son, he might be a good witness. All the rest of the tribe were relieved of further obligation in the matter and advised to go back to their homes, if they had any homes.

Jess Posey was delighted with the prospect of this wonderful excursion. He was eager to see the wondrous outside world. He went feeling certain he would suffer no harm. He felt equally sure the other three would come back in safety.

So the two men, each accompanied by his son, went with the big general to stand trial in the white man's court. One particularly delightful phase of the affair, from Posey's point of view, was that it brought him into the old grizzly's august company for over two weeks. Furthermore, they were to remain together indefinitely; he would be regarded as the old bear's equal.

That grand excursion out to Uncle Sam's court in Salt Lake City was a huge thrill in the lives of the four Paiutes. They did not get tired of telling about it as long as they lived. A hundred thousand people stretched their necks to see them. Instead of suffering unpleasant notoriety they enjoyed popular fame. Their pictures appeared under flamboyant headlines on the front pages of the big dailies. People made a great fuss over them wherever they went. They had abundance of good things to eat and better beds to sleep in than they had ever known before. Besides all this they had a chance to see and enjoy things which their people had never seen nor dreamed of in all their history.

But the most important feature of the trip was that they all came back safe and sound. Not one thing happened to disturb their trusting expectations of peaceful return. The murder and robbery committed on the Ute reservation came under the jurisdiction of the federal court and had to be conducted in Denver. Consequently, Tse-ne-gat had to go to Colorado and stay away a little longer, but this was a welcome extension of his unusual holiday. It gave him more chances to gormandize on rich food, to see picture shows, to go car riding, and to be feasted, and pampered, petted, and indulged nearly to death. Women threw themselves at Tse-ne-gat in Denver. Afterwards he declared he refused propositions of marriage from three of them. For a while he was the most popular man in the big city.

Strangely the court found nothing against the murderous Tse-ne-gat in all the evidence. Even though all the letters and papers taken from Tse-ne-gat were identified by Chacon's wife and parents, the jury found nothing to convict him even though he practically boasted of the awful deed. He was acquitted of all blame. He came back to his people with a most damaging report of Uncle Sam's government and its feeble inability to administer justice.

The misleading reports which had already been brought back by Poke and Posey about the effeminate laws and the effeminate multitude on the outside, were more than confirmed by what Poke's boy had to tell when he got back from Denver, pampered and glutted nearly to death.

It is no exaggeration to say he was pampered and glutted to death in Denver. It was literally true. He survived the inordinate hospitality only a short while after returning to San Juan.

It was reported on the outside that the Paiute war in San Juan was over. It was not. The real trouble patched up temporarily with wretched misunderstandings, was to hang fire for about eight years. Then necessity was to force a fight to a finish. People on the outside, having no idea of actual circumstances in San Juan county, would not believe the true facts even when they were told.

For that matter, the outside world knew nothing about the Paiutes. That is why the posse from the outside failed so miserably. It remained for the settlers who had been born and reared right alongside the Paiutes to handle the situation themselves in the final fight.

Chapter Nineteen

THE BLACK MARE

No one understanding the Paiutes, their beliefs about themselves and their beloved country, looked for any improvement to follow the big excursion. When Posey returned with his happy conclusions, it became clear at once that the truth of the matter would sooner or later have to be brought home to him by a process too stern to be misunderstood.

As if his delusions were not sufficiently unfortunate without further unwarranted interference, a certain society in the eastern states took the trouble to assure Posey, while he was away, that he had endured an unfair deal in San Juan. They told him he must fight for his rights, and they promised to give him assistance. They also sent messengers to him after his return. If there had ever been any possibility of his getting started off on the right foot, these foolish meddlers spoiled that possibility.

Posey returned from the big excursion more convinced than ever before of his immunity from penalties and consequences. He believed the fates would protect him from Uncle Sam, if really Uncle Sam was anything to be feared. He felt sure that these fates would save him from everything and everybody. The big court had sent him back to enjoy complete freedom, even though he had approached an unsuspecting officer under a white flag and had coldly shot him through. Poke too had come back unscathed after killing a representative of the law. As to Tse-ne-gat, all the Paiutes knew what he had done. None of them had ever done anything worse, yet he had been treated like a prince with everything he could eat, or drink, or indulge. He lacked little of urging all his people to go into the killing and robbing business. They would be sure of an excursion and a whale of a time as he had enjoyed.

Posey boasted about immunity, wonderful immunity, The big government had fizzled in its attempt to punish his offenses; the Mormons had shot at him three times and missed; Poke had come after him twice, determined to kill him, and left him alive; Bitseel had got a terrible whipping every time they had collided. No mistake about it. He was untouchable! His every experience was proof of it.

He went so far as to declare that if a bullet were fired straight at him, it would make a detour, or drop to the ground!

But strange to say, he made no big talk about any kind of immunity from his formidable wife—never a threat of deserting or punishing her, no matter how she scolded, belittled, whined, or snarled. Always she had her grizzly brother's image to back her up. Posey had accepted her as the bitter dose of the hard-driven bargain Poke had demanded for Toorah's death. Posey was inclined to abide the conditions—at least while his grizzly brother-in-law continued in robust health.

But Posey had another adversary, an adversary even more dreadful than the second wife. Whether it was real or imaginary he dreaded to think of it. And he never spoke of it. From that day in August 1903 when he was taken handcuffed to jail and when all his camp-neighbors deserted him, leaving him and his family to make their escape alone and he made the humiliating run in nakedness from the river to retreat humbly into exile, Posey had a growing fear of the stern fate meted out by his people to the bad medicine man. Any man disagreeing with the whole tribe was a heretic, a witch, the author of trouble. He might be blamed for any prevailing calamity, and turned on without mercy by his own people.

Woe to the man of whom it was whispered he was the author of calamity. His immediate family and friends were required to become his deadly enemies. It severed their ties of affection, cutting off his kindred in an hour, making him fit only for death.

Bridger Jack, as fine a man as ever the tribe produced, dared to think for himself and to be different from his people. He lost his great influence in just a few days and was shot to ribbons. Kane too, in spite of his bravery and his worth, dared to be unorthodox. He was set upon and killed without ever a word being said about any wrong thing he had done. No escape for the man adjudged to be making bad medicine. They told him nothing; they shot him in the back.

When Posey returned from the big excursion, the bad medicine cloud was far away. No larger than a man's hand. He saw it. It caught his eye in spite of himself. He knew the wind could bring it with deadly increase of size on short notice, yet, so far, he was counting on the bright glow of his immunity.

His faith in immunity was not a thing apart from works. Not at all. The more works, the more immunity. The first thing Posey called for when he returned from the grand excursion was his magnificent long-range gun. His hands had been itching for weeks to hold the treasured weapon again. He fondled it affectionately, looked into the barrel, examined the breech. He resolved to own another just like it. When he heard that a Mexican sheepherder on North Elk had one, he collected his assets for purchase or barter and made the trip successfully.

With the two strong shooters, plus his saddle-gun, his Colt automatic, and his indispensable knife, Posey's became the most formidable arsenal ever acquired by a tribesman. Yet his preparedness was sadly incomplete. He couldn't rest for thinking about it. He must have a "skin-em-all" horse, a tree-smashing, invincible racer to carry him with thunderous bound ahead of the fastest Mormon on the range. He wanted a brute on which he could race away and hide from the last panting pursuer. Some bright day things were going to happen again. He must be mounted on a horse with the mettle and the velocity to lead the "big stir."

He had gone to Dolores for his first trans-canyon gun, and to North Elk for his second. Now where should he go for his trans-country horse? He scrutinized everything he saw under a saddle. Then he began to inquire what kind of horses they had in other parts of the world. He wanted an animal made to order. He was ready to specify the kind of gears, the fibre, the material, the dimensions. He wanted something as tough as a cayuse but not so coyote-like in size. For a real Arabian steed he would have promised all the horses he could steal in the next five years.

Somebody had noticed a few mighty good-looking animals over beyond the big river—somewhere in the neighborhood of Panguitch or Kanab. That sounded good. Anyway there should be something worth while at that distance. So Posey started for Lee's Ferry on the Colorado River. He collected a choice supply of blankets as he crossed the reservation, making sure of a sufficient medium to purchase the best horse he could find.

Toiling on day after day, he rode from the ferry across House-Rock Valley, over the Kaibab Mountains, over the big stretch beyond it, and entered Utah again near Kanab. He sized up everything he saw under saddles, in harnesses, in pastures, or anywhere, eagerly anticipating the imposing form of horse on which he would ride in the lead of the "big stir."

He found it. His judgment of horse-flesh deserved a better cause than the fomenting of more trouble in trouble-weary San Juan. What Posey judged to be the invincible combination of his dreams was a black filly, not yet broken to ride. The number of fine blankets he gave for her indicated how much more than the ordinary horse he took her to be worth.

On her right thigh he burned his brand, P.S. two letters he thought he had learned, although about half the time he got one or both of them backwards. But backwards or forwards, that brand on that black mare meant she was not for sale. Never, never under any circumstances was she to be staked on a game of *ducki!*

CHAPTER TWENTY

MORE *DUCKI*

The lure of *ducki* always drew Posey like a ravenous coyote to a loud-smelling carcass. Though gray hair streaked his temples and he had two little flocks of grandchildren, he was still powerless to resist. He had gone through sorrow from the folly of his ways in general, and through enough shame from his *ducki* in particular, to call for the wisdom and the resolution of penitent reformation. He couldn't reform. Never! Not while he was distracted by the millstone Poke had hung about his neck. The bright-colored cards promised a modicum of respite. They drew him with hypnotic power from the boredom of hearing the eternal nagging of the second wife. *Ducki* was doubly irresistible when it promised a chance to skin the big Navaho.

And the big Navaho, his mop of heavy hair streaked with gray under his greasy little hat, still indulged his passion for the intoxicating game— for the caprice of chance, no matter who shuffled the cards. Even the remotest prospect of trimming his favorite enemy made him drop everything else "short off."

That fall the Navahos staged a big *yabetchi* (festival) on the San Juan below Bluff. They gathered to it from all parts of the reservation. The Paiutes came from the regions northward as far as the Blue and the Elk Mountains. Posey came on his black filly —no thought, of course, to meet Bitseel and have any trouble—no thought, of course, to miss him if there were any chance for them to meet. But Posey did want to display himself on the magnificent creature, the one he would ride in that yet-future glorious chase.

After the main celebration of the *yabetchi*, some tinhorn flashed a deck of cards and a roll of bills. In five minutes a dozen games of *cooncan* were going full swing.

It was inevitable that Posey and the man of the little hat should be bending with watering mouths over the same game. It was equally inevitable that they should be drawn simultaneously into it. Whatever one of them did in the presence of the other was interpreted by that other as a personal dare, or a personal insult, neither of which could ever be allowed to pass without prompt and spirited answer.

When Bitseel, stalwart and stately, but for his contemptible little hat, stooped to lay five cartridges on a black and white card, Posey bent promptly and laid five cartridges against it. They bet again and still again doubling the amount. Those halfdozen thrusts looked mild enough, but each one, whether he realized it or not, was simply sparring for an opening. The tenth bet assumed rather heavy proportions and the Paiute won.

Boast and banter are the sweet sap of *ducki*, but Bitseel had admired the professional poker-player's technique of hiding his feelings behind a bronze mask of stoical silence—at least until his feelings became so volcanic they brust forth like hot lava. So far in this battle he had not spoken a word. Yet, nettled by his bad luck, he threw down a bet amounting in value twice what he had lost. "Skunk-bait!" he hissed as he spread his silver on the blanket.

Posey flinched. That ugly expression smelled strongly of bad medicine. It had been followed before by immediate disaster to him. Worse still, it was intended as an insult, and it always jabbed him in the sorest place. In nervous resentment he hunted the necessary amount from his disordered pockets and stacked it with clench-jawed rancor against the big bet. "Coyote-medicine!" he snarled, as antitoxin to Bitseel's poison.

Since to the Navahos the word *coyote* means thief, Bitseel took this as an personal insult and sent a fierce glare at his antagonist. But the next flip of the cards gave him the big stake, and he raked it in with silent exultation.

Immediate disaster again after the Navaho's mysterious curse! Would Posey yield in fear? Not a bit of it. With his next bet he would stress his own curse with unfailing malice.

The skunk and the coyote elbowed their way into opposite seats at the blanket. After they eliminated all the original players, each determined to eliminate the other.

The skunk's curse was futile. All its heart-burning emphasis was in vain. He lost steadily: his money, his proud hat, his dagger-like knife, and the worst yet, his new lariat! He loosed it from his saddle on the black mare and handed it over with anguish to his poker-faced enemy. Pride and anger demanded that he carry on with the game, so he explained that he had a horse worth thirty dollars, which he would stake on three ten-dollar bets. The game went on with Posey using matches to represent dollars.

The coyote got all thirty matches, counted them before the feverish eyes of the skunk, arose and started to take possession of the black mare.

What was he doing! Nothing had been said about the black mare—she was not at all the animal that the skunk had staked.

The hell she wasn't! Then why hadn't he made that clear? the coyote wanted to know. He had! To any one with a grain of sense, the skunk shot back.

At that the big Navaho began loosening the laragos to remove the saddle, intending to take for himself at a figure of thirty dollars, the special colt of destiny for which Posey had made a three-hundred-mile trip and paid a figure so high he was ashamed to tell it.

Old Tsabekiss himself and a whole caravan of kinsmen were in attendance at the *yabetchi* in formidable array. A prolonged scuffle and a hair-pulling would bring them quick to the scene. No telling what would happen to the black mare before it was settled. Snatching his automatic from under his arm, the skunk struck the coyote a quick blow in the face, leaped to his saddle and dashed for cover.

Bitseel staggered and fell. A quick howl of alarm sounded and a dozen Navahos mounted up in haste and whipped away in hot pursuit of the flying Paiute. There was dust and din and commotion, but the black filly left them all behind and disappeared in the faraway. She was proving herself fit for a time when Posey would repose in her the greatest confidence he had ever reposed in any horse. Riding the mare cheered Posey a bit. He began to console himself; Even if he had lost his money, his hat, his rope, his knife, yet he still had his gun and the wonderful flying filly. He would meet the coyote no more. Neither would he ever pay the debt about which he had been so basely injured.

That dozen Navahos returned from their futile effort to catch the black mare. They knew better than to follow on into the rocks. When they considered that their tribesman had only been knocked down, and that it was just a quarrel over a card-game—the flare-up of an old sore, and that the blow was probably more of an insult than an injury, they resigned it to parties of the fuss to fight it out in their own way.

Bitseel's high check-bone was caved in by that blow with the automatic. It gave him pain for weeks and left an ugly dent across his face. He never recovered his former appearance. While he nursed his aching face he resolved—and fate decreed—that he and the skunk should meet once more—only once more.

This latest fracas did not cause any serious breach between Posey and the people of the southern tribe. He went among them when he pleased as before, even as far as Kayenta. But he steered clear of the man who carried the mark of his automatic.

CHAPTER TWENTY-ONE

GENERAL POSEY

The white ashes of the fires of La Sal and Soldier Crossing had blown with the wind nearly forty years before. But, somehow, they still burned bright in Posey's eager imagination. In fact, they burned brighter there every year. They needed no fanning from the second wife or from anybody else. But in telling him eternally how her grizzly old brother would do it and therefore how he should do it, the second wife was fanning a dangerous flame. But the flame of former Paiute glory was something which Posey fanned for himself. In his dreams—and in his daydreams—he rode the black mare in the lead of his people over the Trail of the Fathers.

He had definitely eliminated Uncle Sam from the enemies he had once feared. Strangers from the outside world were still sending him assurance, urging him to yield nothing. His people had only to throw off the local government administered by the Mormons and they would be as free as they were when they howled their challenge centuries before from the beetling rim of Elk Mountain and from the high shelf over Soldier Crossing.

With his assured immunity from every missile of death —with his matchless black mare and his long-range guns Posey was certain that he would lead his people in glory to their former greatness. They would take the Old Trail again. No one would dare to follow them. They would glut on the fat of the land while their enemies cowered in some gulch or sneaked away in the night.

Some of the old men shook their heads as they contemplated Posey's fantastic notions. Sometimes the force of their objections seemed to Posey dangerously like the little hand-sized cloud which he had imagined he saw on the horizon. He recalled with a chill the fate of Bridger Jack and Kane, and others who had strayed too far from the thinking of the tribe. So Posey carefully refrained from dwelling on these things when the older men were within hearing. But he still repeated in Blanding his notion of his charmed life, declaring that no bullets could touch him.

His story of a rousing big fight, the Old Trail, and plunder galore, sold like hot cakes to a snarl of adolescent incorrigibles. Joe Bishop's three boys, Dutchie's boys, young Sanop's outlaw sons, and others of their class went wild over Posey's pictures of the coming big stir. Inflamed and fired by glowing accounts of horror and glory, they began an alarming program of depredation. They shot down cattle, burned bridges, maimed horses, and otherwise defied the law. When one of them was arrested in Bluff, Posey went to the sheriff with terrible threats, declaring that the tribe would go again on the war-path, make a big slaughter, and take a tremendous spoil.

Among Posey's ardent and irresponsible followers was Pahneab, the second son of Joe Bishop. (This Joe Bishop was no relation to Poke's brother.) Posey found Pahneab an eager listenser to the stories of war and glory. He proceeded to inflame the youngster's fancies, which needed at this time, most of all, to be modified.

No semblance of discipline ever entered into the mutinous life of Pahneab. From the days of his infancy, he despised all restraint. If Posey had known

a fraction as much about men as he knew about
horses, he would have reposed no trust whatever in
this wildbrained youth. That he ever did trust Pah-
neah is a great wonder for he had ample opportunity
to see and know Joe Bishop's son was a born anarchist.

Yet Posey took pains to coach this violent hoodlum,
with others of his kind, for the occasion of the future
uprising. He even planned a sham surprise on a company of cowmen going from Blanding to Elk Mountain, thinking in this way to give his youthful recruits
somewhat of an idea of action under his command.
They were to make their sudden appearance on every
side of the white men, but instead of an attack, as in
the day of the coming stir, after they had made the
surprise, they must pass it off as a joke and let the
cowmen go on with a laugh to disguise the real purpose of the maneuver.

But Pahneab, when he had helped spring the sham
surprise, flew viciously at one of the cowmen, Corey
Perkins. He struck him fiercely on the head with a
quirt and, snatching his gun from his scabbard, swore
he would kill him right there. That is apparently what
he would have done if General Posey had not made
quick and firm interference. He had to talk to the
boy as he would to a dog to make him put his gun away
and be quiet. Posey made a poor and embarrassed
effort to explain. He hoped it would not be misunderstood—he hoped too that it would not be told. The
whole sorry situation was a startling reminder to
Posey that he was not as near ready as he had supposed. Pahneab in particular would require more careful drilling.

In spite of the wise old men and the conservatives
of the tribe, Posey's enthusiasm was contagious like
a pleasing refrain which people find themselves sing-

ing before they are aware. For one thing they had
all been charmed by the notion of the big gun, and
with no incentive but the novelty of its unusual charm,
they began to buy it whenever they could. It became
popular to have one—and first thing they knew it had
started many of them on Posey's way of thinking.
They were being lead blindly by a bad-medicine man.
The bad-medicine man himself lived in growing dread
of the cloud-sized evil his bad medicine was bound
to loose upon him.

With the opening of the year 1923, prospects looked
favorable for aggravating troubles leading to a big
stir. Nearly every man of the tribe was well armed
and had a good horse. There was less dissension among
them than for a long time past, and nearly all the
tribe were camped together among the cedars a mile
west of Blanding. Since Poke had withdrawn from
them in a kind of disgust or sorrow following the death
of his notorious son, Tse-ne-gat, and had made his
camp on the state line near Yellow Jacket, Posey was
free to develop his plans with less hindrance.

He could give nothing like an order to his people,
yet he was swaying them by his example. In this way
he had been influential in having them camped just
a mile from town among the thick trees and the rocks.
The rugged little gulch, yawning between their camps
and the town, gave them the advantage of being near
enough to see what was going on, and still far enough
away to be sufficiently out of sight for quick disappearance.

Posey had employed a Navaho silversmith to make
a silver star out of a dollar. He wore this on his vest
indicating the rank of captain he wanted to hold or
possibly the rank he thought he did hold. For fifty
years he had cherished an ambition to have a brist-

ling mustache straight up and down across his mouth,
but he had matured only sixteen lonesome hairs on
each side giving him a kind of catfish appearance.
However, he did wear a wide black hat like Poke had
always worn, and he cherished the belief that Poke's
mantle of leadership had fallen on him. To himself
he was General Posey.

Already some of the more energetic men of the
camp had gone to work at the shearing pens and elsewhere. Soon the tribe might be too widely scattered
for any kind of concerted action. Posey inspired Pahneab and other scoff-laws to acts of thrilling depre-
dations which he thought would surely provoke some
kind of lively response, but they got little attention—
the people had grown tired of trying to prosecute
them.

To General Posey it was discouraging. Soon spring
would be gone, his people scattered, and nothing
started. He would try again. He encouraged Pahneab
and two of Dutchie's boys to hold up a sheep camp at
the point of gun and help themselves to whatever
appealed to their fancy. Surely this would incite the
white men to some positive action and get the real fun
underway. Posey waited hopefully to begin hostilities
as soon as the law officers would start playing their
part of the exciting game.

But it took some time for that sheepherder to report
the robbery to his boss, and then the boss was delayed
in reporting to the owner. When the owner finally got
around to the justice of the peace and swore out a
complaint and put it in the hands of sheriff Bill Oliver,
the Paiutes had relaxed their vigilance and what happened took them by surprise.

Bill Oliver, without delay or ceremony, hunted up
the boys, two of them, and took them into custody

when they had all but forgotten the incident. Without any unnecessary preliminaries the two boys were taken into court. The whole thing was maturing very differently to what the general had intended.

This peremptory arrest and speedy trial of the fire-eating Pahneab had come and caught Posey napping. He learned that the trial was being conducted in the bsaement of one of the school-buildings in town. Mounting his black mare he came on the run. He left the mare at the head of the steps and marched down into the court, Lochinvar style, with bold contempt for the procedure and all those present. Making his way boldly to a seat near to his dear disciples, he began with whispered grunts and signs to familiarize Pahneab with his plans for his escape. The court tolerated Posey as an ignorant intruder. No one could understand his guttural grunts and signs and no one suspected the desperate nature of his visit.

Pahneab pretended to be lame, very lame! He carried with him a great thick stick on which he leaned heavily. There was little else for him to do in the crowded room except to make some kind of answer to the questions asked. He placed all the blame on Dutchie's boy who was still at large. He pretended not to hear much of what was said to him, although he had heard every grunt from his anxious general. At noon this houseful of men would go home for dinner—Posey would wait with his mare near the top of the steps—Pahneab would pretend that his lame leg was numb from sitting so long and he would delay there as long as possible till the room was cleared. No one but the Paiutes comprehended this outline of the plan, but they got it in detail.

When the court adjourned for dinner, Posey hurried to the black mare, as agreed. Much hung in suspense on these few minutes. He watched fearfully. Sheriff Oliver, impatient at the delay of his prisoners, preceded them to the top of the stone steps, calling to them to come and go with him to dinner. Pahneab made poor progress, being very lame. The sheriff moved near to his sorrel horse ready to mount, expecting the two Indians to walk ahead of him.

Suddenly Pahneab was no longer lame. He leaped quickly at the sheriff, striking at him with the big stick, but Oliver had just risen in one stirrup, and the blow fell on the horse. Having missed his lick Pahneab leaped to the back of the waiting black mare. He was turning her to run when Sheriff Oliver spurred his horse quickly and seized the mare's bit.

Pahneab countered this movement by snatching Oliver's pistol from its holster and thrusting it against his breast. His intentions were deadly. He pulled the trigger. The hammer clicked on a cartridge but it failed to discharge! Oliver later declared that his pistol had never misfired before.

Though Pahneab failed to kill the sheriff, he did give him such a start that he released his grip on the mare's reins. As soon as the mare's head was free, the wild youth started off on a keen jump. As he went he snapped that gun again in Oliver's direction. This time it fired, striking the sorrel horse in the neck.

The black mare flew like a streak. Dutchie's boy vanished. Posey fled cross-lots to the camps. Most of the men who had been in court attending the hearing were out of sight. Those near enough to see the break had no guns and could do nothing worthwhile in the way of immediate interference.

Oliver dashed home for his rifle and pursued the black mare till she disappeared with her rider among the trees and rocks. To follow would be suicide.

CHAPTER TWENTY-TWO

THE BIG STIR

The big stir was on! It had come as the sharp crack of a whip, and it found most of the Paiutes lounging around the stores or killing time at other places in town. Many of them knew nothing of what had happened.

When Posey and *Dutchie To-ats* (Dutchie's boy) ran panting into camp beyond West Water, everything was in an uproar at once. Pahneab had dashed by on the black mare and was bringing the horses in from the sagebrush flat beyond. They must be gone! No time to lose! Posey dared now to give imperious orders.

But the Paiutes in camp objected that most of their people were not there—they were still in town. Parts of families there at the wickiups fumed and cried for children or wives or fathers or brothers still in Blanding. The sheriff had turned back, but he would get help and be after them.

Then some of their people arrived breathless from town—wild, terrified. They reported that every man in Blanding was running for his gun— getting horses to ride—any horse in sight, the very first they could find.

Pahneab came pell-mell with the ponies from the flat. Everybody in camp ran to get his rope on his animal, to pack up and be gone. Teegre sprang to the back of his buckskin and raced away to the east rim of West Water gulch at the edge of town. There he called in long and penetrating tones to his people. *"Woo-eeh-eeh! Tospon pikey! Tooish apane!"*

His magnificent voice carried far through the cool spring air. But the Paiutes in town, though they heard, had been hurriedly rounded up by determined men who held them in a body and ordered them not to move a step.

As Teegre returned at breakneck speed, heavy Joe Bishop, perspiring and panting from undue haste, came dragging up from West Water. He reported that he was the last man to escape the roundup in town. Fifty or more of their people were prisoners—men standing over them with guns. No use for those in the camp to wait for any of their people in town any longer.

Impotent haste and frightened confusion reigned in camp. Fear-stricken Indians cinched saddles on squirming, protesting cayuses. They piled beds and provisions and supplies on the saddles in bunglesome heaps. They urged their motley flocks of goats up from the groves of oak in the canyon, expecting every minute to be attacked by the men from the town.

They must be off! *"Tooish apane! Tooish apane!"* commanded General Posey impatiently.

A few old Paiutes protested. How could they start on the Old Trail with half of their people held prisoner in town? How could they desert them? Possibly they would be kept as hostages pending the outcome of the trouble.

No difference! They must go! At once! Posey would come back in the night and get the prisoners. That was a promise. *"Tooish apane!"*

They mounted in a panic and headed wildly for the nearest cover of thick trees and rocks to the south. Joe Bishop, puffing and palpitating with his fat, and trying to get his saddle on his fidgeting pony, was left behind. He was still trying to get the saddle on that loco cayuse when Sheriff Oliver and other armed men rode into camp.

"Where's your boy?" demanded Oliver.

"I show you," Old Joe panted. Getting his ponderous weight at last into the saddle, he started on the reeking trail of his people, with the white men at his heels.

Pahneab's father had no intention of giving his son away. He figured that once among the thick trees he could dodge out of sight. Then hurrying forward to his people, he could tell them how many were in pursuit. When he dodged, Dave Black dodged after him, jabbing him fiercely in the ribs with the muzzle of his gun to convince him that the only way to save his life was to cooperate or return to the roundup in Blanding.

Two miles down West Water Point, Posey and his fugitives stopped to consider. Which way should they go? At what point should they enter The Big Trail? The Big Trail was to the west. General Posey wanted to turn that way at once. He was met again by the popular objection about the people held in town. The best fighters of the tribe were there, including Scotty. And they should by all means have Poke to be their leader!

Poke for their leader! The very idea of it after all that Posey had done for them! His blood boiled.

The inevitable second wife was loud with the popular majority, making veiled threats of what her brother would do if he were left out. Also, a-plenty would happen to them if they tried to carry on the big push without him. The fleeing band lacked little of mutiny right there and then.

Posey knew they must go on in spite of everything. They must go on even if he had to yield a point. He did yield a point right there, a very dear point, amounting almost to the abdication of his imperial ambition. He yielded to their request that a messenger be sent to Poke, telling him to meet them. Accordingly, instead of turning to the west and getting nearer to the Old Trail, they turned east for a point on Recapture where the old grizzly was to join them.

Posey recognized the advantage of having Poke with them. He knew that one grunt from the old grizzly was worth more than forty ordinary fighting men. If he could come as one of Posey's lieutenants, that would be wonderful, but Posey resisted the idea of having his brother-in-law supersede him. Hitherto Poke, more than any other man in the tribe, had been the author of all the big fights. And Posey had got a place in them only by inviting himself. And he had had to march in the mean tail of the procession. Now, as prime mover of this big event, he had a great ambition to invite the tough old bear to occupy a place in the ranks behind him.

After that mutinous display on West Water Point, and with half his people under arrest, and with that second wife spluttering around like a hen with one chicken, Posey thought he would be delighted to have the old grizzly's help in organizing the whole infernal mess. As the brains of the riproaring wars, and with at least seven men to his credit, Poke could paw this mutinous herd into line and compell every man to do his "ragged damndest."

The messenger left at once for Yellow Jacket, leaning forward on his speeding horse. The rest of the fugitives pushed on after him towards Recapture. Later in the afternoon they stopped to take a much-needed lunch at an old cabin on Murphy Point.

In ten minutes Sheriff Oliver and his posse appeared at a field gate to the north of them. The posse was rather too far away for a shot, but Posey plowed up the dust in front of them as a hint to slow down. The Paiutes, taking shelter behind the cabin, rushed their refreshments onto the fire. When those items of food had no more than begun to sizzle, they saw a greater posse joining Oliver and coming through the gate.

Posey's people might stop somewhere later on, but not there. They must be moving. Some of them, ravenous with hunger, gulped part of their half-cooked victuals with swine-like dispatch, throwing the rest away and piling their loads back onto the horses in a terrible jumble.

To hold their course toward Recapture now, meant to meet the posse in the open. That simply couldn't be— it was contrary to the very first principles of their warfare. They would have to go back. One more distressing development! The whistle of bullets admonished them that the posse had guns as big as their own.

"What about my brother?" whined the second wife. "What can we ever do without him?" She hesitated as if she would go on at all hazards to Recapture.

"To hell with your brother!" roared the distracted Posey. "It's easier for him to come to us, than for all of us to go to him."

It was not possible for them to know it that day —and certain ones of them were to die before it could be reported that Poke listened with nothing but disgust to Posey's messenger. He grunted, *"Pu-neeh!* He learns no more than a skunk and they will kill him for making such a big stink."

After that the old grizzly packed up and moved farther away into Colorado, camping near a ranch in McElmo. There he had a chance to hear about the fight without being near enough to be blamed or praised for the nature of its outcome.

Three squaws and two papooses in Posey's outfit were so sure that Poke was their only hope of deliverance that they dropped out of the company on Murphy Point. Later they were found hiding in a cave half-way to Yellow Jacket.

Posey and his people, keeping out of sight behind the Murphy cabin, hurried west for the nearest rocks. There in the rim of White Mesa Canyon their snipers hid to cover their retreat. The main company rode lash and lather down through the rocks to the west side.

Posey's people descended the canyon on the lope, treading one on another's heels and jostling violently at every turn in the trail. Posey lay watching the little notch in the rim through which the posse would come off the point. He resolved to bore the first man through who came in sight.

At that first man of the posse, who happened to be John D. Rogers, he let fly with his big gun, expecting to cut his man through the lungs from the side. Crack-shot though he was, from long and careful practice, his bullet went low. Barely grazing John's hip-pocket, it pierced the tree of the saddle and broke the backbone of the horse.

When Posey saw the horse drop, and the rider leap from sight and no one else appear, he craned his neck to scan that vicinity, and incidentally to look behind and to each side. Off to the north he discovered a car coming from the distance to head his people from crossing the road on the west side of the canyon. He

crept around hurriedly to a position from which he
could rake the seats of that Model T as it passed,
waiting eagerly while it sped nearer. Three men occupied the back seat, two the front.

Two shots should finish the five of them. In spite
of his bead on the coveted prize his first shot pierced
the car just back of the men in the rear seat. Four
inches further ahead and it would have gone through
the lungs of Warren Allan, George Hurst and Frank
Redd.

Of course, Posey knew nothing of how far he had
missed. He only knew that the little car rattled right
on. In a very few seconds it would be out of range. So
he aimed for a wheel and punctured a tire. The machine wobbled and stopped in an open space where no
rocks or banks could shield it from him. Now he would
blow its passengers into ribbons.

Within a few seconds, the five men would have
been Posey's game if John Rogers and Leland Redd
had not seen the smoke from his sniper's nest. They
made life so perilous in that nest that Posey leaped
headlong from it and rushed away to join his people
before he was cut off from them.

Later that March afternoon the fleeing fugitives
approached Ruin Spring, nine miles southwest of
Blanding. There they appropriated six horses running
in a field. This represented all the plunder of the "big
stir" thus far.

Some time after their turn back toward the west,
they were joined again by their herd of goats. Although
these long-legged Paiute goats can travel a long way
on the run, they hindered the speed of this rag-shag
flying company. As the bedraggled Paiutes bolted
down the narrows of Ruin Spring Canyon, their
children began whimpering for food and their panting

goats threatened to go on strike. General Posey and his special aide stopped there behind the rocks to way-lay anyone who might disturb the outfit while they made camp in Cottonwood. But the posse made no attempt to follow into the canyon, and in the early evening the ambuscade moved on to join the camp.

They had started now toward The Big Trail. Every mile in that direction should give them added se-curity. Soon they would reach a point where no one would dare to follow —a point beyond which no pur-suer had ever survived. But what about their people held under guard in town? What about the gallant braves kept shamefully in prison in Blanding? General Posey had promised to accomplish their rescue that night. He knew they all expected it from him and he cudgled his brain for a way to accomplish the seem-ingly-impossible.

After instructing his people to start before dawn and to wait for him in the Butler, Posey left their camp in the Cottonwood. He rode off into the night, sworn to find a way to do the thing on which not only his toleration as leader but his very life hung as by a frail thread. That hand-sized cloud which he had seen on the distant horizon, looked dark and threat-ening. It was imperative that the rest of their people be with them, or how could they go in victory on the Old Trail?

Somewhere in the territory his people had traversed that afternoon, the posse would be waiting for the dawn. Posey would hazard no chance of finding them, so he took his way up the winding course of the Cotton-wood, and then along an old wagon road leading out by Three Cedars.

He expected to find the prisoners guarded at some open camp in the streets of town, their guards in plain

view and at the mercy of anyone who might shoot at
them from the darkness. Instead, when he rode
cautiously into the sleeping town, he saw but one light,
and that was in the basement of the school house.
Approaching with great care he discovered that armed
guards stood at various places outside. Others, no
doubt, were watching from dark windows above. Unless he kept at a distance he would be seen.

BROKEN CHARM

Chapter Twenty-three

What possible chance had Posey to effect the escape of his tribesmen? He could plunge the whole situation into quick excitement and confusion. But what would that accomplish? Some of his people might be killed and any of the guards would stand a good chance of shooting him or his mare, once his presence was known.

It was a hopeless case. He burned with dread and shame for the white-feather report he would have to make to his people. Since he had promised to see Jack Fly, Jim Mike, and other Paiutes tending sheep in the upper fields, and since he had ridden far and the night was already well spent, he hurried away to have it over with before the dawn.

Finding three of his people at the sheep-camp, he told them of the wild state of affairs and ordered them to make it known to all the others they could find. Then he loped off to the southwest as an unwelcome nimbus began to show on the eastern horizon.

Daylight found the fugitives crossing Black Mesa and the posse sniffing their trail out of Cottonwood. In the absence of his general the rattle-brained Pahneab had plenty to say about their policy of action. Teegre and Anson Posey wrestled with the problem of averting disaster into which he threatened to plunge them.

The second wife, peeved that they had not waited for her brother according to plan, refused to be quieted. Mutinous rumblings from within the company boded more harm to them that anything they could see from without. Why in reason didn't Posey come? He was to have joined them in the Butler, bringing with him the prisoners from town. Here they were still in the Butler with that persistent pack of Mormons determinedly close behind them. Without their leader to handle the crisis they grew uneasy.

Not knowing what else to do and with only advisers like Pahneab to direct them, they climbed westward from the Valley of the Butler to the sharp rim overlooking the Comb Wash. There they camped on a lofty point, or eagle's nest, from which they could scan the country in all directions.

Though it was still early in the day, they fumed at the delay and uncertainty. Surely something had gone wrong with Posey's rescue plan. After what he had done they might shoot him on first sight. Maybe they had seen him.

The Butler and the Comb run southward in an unusual parallel for thirty miles. They are nowhere more than three miles apart, with only three places where it is possible to go from one over into the other. The east wall of the Comb is smooth and all but perpendicular. From its knife-like top the bare, cavernous rock slopes down eastward to the bottom of the Butler.

By the direction of Pahneab, or someone equally fruitful in fool's notions, the Paiutes had stopped on a reef to one side of a pass into the Comb, never thinking how easily they could be hemmed off from escape. In that dangerous place they sat down to wait for General Posey's reinforcements— the company of prisoners he had promised to liberate and bring with him.

Down over their trail from Black Mesa on the east they saw the posse coming like wolves to get them. The dangerous elements within their own ranks began to seethe with suicidal heat. Their war-spirit contended with fear, their unity with mutiny.

With murderous intent they sent three of their number to lie in ambush under the tall brush where the trail crosses the wash in the bottom of the valley. It was a clever plan, with Anson Posey as the leader. The three hid where they could sweep the main trail with their bullets, spreading death if the posse should come that way. They waited in vain.

Dave Black, captain of the posse, ordered his men to stay out of the wash. Instead they would make their crossing above and get around to the west. There they got a glimpse of the three waiting in ambush, though not soon enough to shoot. The snipers, sensing by instinct that they had been spotted, scrambled off into the wash and barely escaped being cut off from returning to the main band at the eagle's nest above them.

Most of the men of the posse were afoot on the west side. Although there was much bald, dangerous rock there, Posey thought his invincible mare would be more than a match for the men without horses.

That west side was sliced by hundreds of little box-canyons. When Posey started up the slope, behold, one of these canyons ran between him and Black's men. Dave Black and his brother Morley ran up along the south side of the little gulch, firing at Posey as he raced along the north side firing at them. The gulch turned out to be so irregular and crooked, with so many little tributaries too deep for a horse, that the men afoot had the advantage. The skin-em-all mare, panting and wheezing for breath, fell farther behind as the race proceeded.

In this race Posey was not sitting erect in the saddle as an accommodating target. He hung low on the mare's right side, firing from under her neck, thus using her body as a stop for any bullet coming his way. His left hip, silhouetted in the saddle against the sky, was the target these sporting pursuers shot at, instead of at the faithful mare.

As Posey raced up along that gulch, the wondrous immunity about which he had marveled and boasted, was suspended, at least for a brief interval. Two of the bullets failed to make a detour around him. Both struck him in that exposed hip one inflicting only a flesh-wound, the other cutting more deeply, and grazing the bone.

With no possibility of reaching the top in safety, Posey whirled away to the north, concealing himself among the trees along the rim. It was a long way to the next pass above there into the Comb, but his only hope was to go that way and come back down the bottom on the west side. Then he could climb the trail to the south and come back along the knife-edge to the eagle's nest.

By that upper trail he lay waiting a long time in torture, hoping vengefully that some of the posse would follow and give him a chance to even the score. Until late in the afternoon he hugged that ambush, but no one came.

None of Black's men had time to follow Posey. He had no more than disappeared when Jack Fly, Jim Mike, and the other man whom Posey had aroused at the sheep camp that night, appeared up the valley. They were in a threatening position to get the horses of the posse in the bottom of the valley unless a delegation hurried to the foot of the hill to head them off.

Leaving Bill Young to guard the top of the reef, and to head Posey if he tried to return, the two Black brothers started for the bottom. Morley hurried ahead, only to find himself in the fight alone. Jack Fly and Jim Mike fired at him from the wash, where they peered over the sandy rim under the brush. They were at close range. Fly was a crack-shot, but he missed every time. Surely there was bad medicine somewhere! Jack had never done such slovenly shooting before. That white man had a charmed life!

Fly had fired three times before Dave Black arrived on the scene and erased all doubt in the minds of either Jack or Jim as to whether or not Morley and himself had charmed lives. Dave had crept up to where he could see Jack making ready to fire again, and Jim was about to try his luck. Dave shot Jack's big hat off his head, barely missing his skull and filling his eyes full of grit from the sandbank over which he had been peering. Then Dave and Morley shot at the same time, making two holes through Jim's blanket, but only grazing the skin under his arm.

That was enough for Mike! It looked so much like bad medicine that he and Jack, followed by their companion, threw themselves backwards into the wash, mounted on their cayuses and rode for dear life. They left Jack's hat and Mike's blanket right there and followed the crooked course of the wash a mile before they ventured to look out.

Assuring themselves that they were not within reach of the posse's guns, the three found a way out the east side of that wash and climbed the rim of Black Mesa, hunting for a safety zone. They never came back to the fight. They represented the total reinforcement Posey had gained by his long ride in the night, and they contributed nothing to his cause.

The roar of Jack Fly's big gun and the roar of the other guns spread excitement in the eagle's nest where

Pahneab was champing the bits and cursing all advice to stay in camp. He and Dutchie To-ats, his fellow-defendant in the trial, dashed off in contempt of all restraint. They intended to clear a way for their general to come back along the reef to camp. Discovering Bill Young alone on the rim, they fired at him from a distance and started to run him down.

Bill had already begun to dodge from cover to cover for the purpose of joining the men below to find out the cause of the commotion. Suddenly he was aware that the Indians were shooting his way and were approaching him horse-back on the run. He hurried to a point where he could get behind a thick cedar, watching their movements while he rested his gun through a fork of the limbs.

They were coming on the lope, guns in their hands, headed straight for the place where they had seen him last. They intended to ride one on each side of his cedar.

Bill knew the supreme moment had come either for him or for them, or possibly for one of them and then for him. No time now to juggle with fine distinctions and fussy sentiments. When their break-neck speed had brought them within thirty feet, Bill took a bead on a button of Pahneab's greasy shirt-front and fired. Reloading in the fewest possible seconds he was ready for what had to be done next.

Pahneab drew up in a convulsed knot and uttered a choking malediction, (Son em a—)" But his voice trailed off with sinking emphasis and he fell in a writhing heap to the sand.

Dutchie To-ats whirled his horse and whipped to get out of sight. Bill held a fine bead on his back and had a perfect chance to bore him through, but he saw no need and had no appetite to shoot again. The way

Pahneab had fallen dead in a fit was a sight Bill had no wish ever to see repeated.

The dead Paiute's pony stopped short and waited there faithfully for his master to rise, while Dutchie called loudly from beyond the hill, unwilling to decide that he would never get an answer.

Later in the day a young man of the posse took Pahneab's hat as a trophy. Still later some of the Paiutes came down and got Pahneab's gun, his horse, and his other valuables, and left his body to puff up there in the heat. After the fight, some of the posse dug a hole by it, pushed it in, and covered it over.

The fight went on fitfully into late afternoon, both sides shooting from under cover and to poor advantage. Three Indian ponies fell under fire, one of them crumpling right under his master who was riding for cover.

Finally Black's men quit firing. A strange, ominous silence seemed to prevail. The people in the eagle's nest took it to mean they were about to be hemmed off by stealth of the enemy, with no possible escape but to plunge over the dizzy cliff into the Comb.

Seized with panic they stampeded. Running madly along the rim they left everything, simply springing to their saddles and going on the keen jump. They had brought their goats with them to this point, but now these creatures were left to hunt browse where they would.

The posse ceased firing to determine their next move. Holding council in a sheltered place, they knew nothing of what was happening above them. They decided to go home, equip for the job, and return early prepared to fight it out to a finish.

When the posse returned to town they rode up to the guards at the school house. The Paiute prisoners were staring apprehensively through the basement windows. Joe Bishop recognized Pahneab's hat tied on one of the saddles. Without waiting to hear what had happened, he guessed that his son had been killed. He uttered a long bitter cry like a broken-hearted child, sobbing with the abandon of grief seldom heard from a man. No one who heard it felt anything but pity, for Joe Bishop was never a bad man.

CHAPTER TWENTY-FOUR

BAD MEDICINE

His hip aching fiendishly, Posey hung doggedly to that ambush at the upper Comb trail till late in the afternoon. At last he decided it was useless to wait longer, descended west to the bottom, intent on reaching the eagle's nest by way of the lower trail. He met his people hurtling wildly up the wash; they had barely escaped being surrounded—better come! quick! No time to stop and talk!

Posey needed no coaxing. Urging their weary animals forward, they turned up Mule Creek, west of Comb Wash in the early evening. Before dark they reached a small butte with steep and vertical rock on all sides. If they could get on top of that island hill, they could defend themselves from all comers. In feverish haste they began to build a rude trail up the northeast side of that butte.

Sometime in the weary hours of the night they found themselves on top the butte with nothing to eat, and no blankets in which to rest, no goats to milk nor to butcher. What in the world could they do? Possibly, after all, the eagle's nest was not surrounded. Even if Black's men had surrounded it, they would have found it empty and gone away. In any case, the Paiutes had to have something to eat, even if they had to rob Karnell's ranch just above the mouth of Mule Creek. Before going to the ranch, however, they would see if their stuff still remained on the rock.

It was a rough night with black clouds, moaning winds, and fitful gusts of snow. Snow would add to their misery. Worse still, it would advertise their movements in a trail behind them as plain as a black mark on white paper.

Leaving a few squaws on the island to care for the little papooses, the rest of the band descended through the darkness and storm over their new trail, down Mule Creek, and down Comb Wash. They struggled to reach the eagle's nest in the minimum of time, lest morning light should disclose them in the dangerous open.

A miserable wind whistling up Comb Wash drove snow in their faces. Peril waited for them in every step their horses took on the slippery wet reef. Nothing had been taken from their camp. They found most of their goats, packed up their stuff, and reached the top of the butte again soon after dawn of the wintry morning. Sure enough, their back trail through the sift of snow was a dark line on a white surface.

Were they to fight here on this island-rock? What if it were surrounded? This island was dry as a bone. Eventually they would have to surrender or choke to death.

Yes, the general insisted. They would fight right here. They would soon use up the small party that had been dogging them the last two days. Then, before a greater number could collect, they would have their feet on the impregnable Trail of their Fathers.

They began preparing a rather pretentious breakfast: meat, coffee, hot bread, stewed fruit and other side dishes, for this was about the first chance they had had to eat in safety since the trouble began. Yet they wrangled and quarreled and neglected the cooking. Posey saw the mutinous dregs of the tribe boiling up in sickly colors to the surface. The second wife loomed big among those yellow dregs.

"This fight talk is crazy!" she insisted, with unusual authority in her whining old voice, for she knew
she expressed the sentiment of the majority. "If my
brother were here he would see what is the best thing
for us to do. Posey always does things the wrong way."

"They can shoot us here and we can't get at them,"
whimpered Dutchie-Toats, his blood still frozen to
strawberry ice with the recollection of Pahneab's last
yell.

Others, on whom Posey had depended, sided with
his mutinous wife, for really, if the chief couldn't
command his squaw, how could he command them?
Everybody took part in the quarrel. It occupied not
only their time but their attention while the meat and
bread burned.

Then a boy in a terrified yell called their attention
to a company of twenty horsemen coming up the Comb.
This unexpected increase in the ranks of their enemy
gave them a new chill. So far they had failed to make
a single shot tell a decent story. On top of that, they
had lost a man, and Posey himself was painfully
wounded in spite of his professed immunity. It looked
awfully bad. Something in the unremitting and careful
resolution of these Mormons reminded the Paiutes
of that long ago when they had marched Posey per-
emptorily out of his wickiup and compelled him at last
to sue for peace. Breakfast was all but forgotten.
Squaws cried, men grew sullen. The second wife in
I-told-you-so tones declared that all this had resulted
from their running away from her brother after they
had promised to meet him.

Then another terrified yell vibrated with freezing
echo into their systems. A squaw pointed to twenty
more mounted white men coming down the Comb towards the mouth of Mule Creek where the first twenty

were waiting. Apparently one company had come from Bluff, the other from Blanding. The forty men headed up the creek toward them. A strange anxiety covered the island. No one had any appetite for any part of the breakfast salvaged from the fire.

Posey insisted they must fight. Sore and embittered, and numb with pain, he burned with a feverish lust to shoot, to cut, to strike death-blows right and left. His war talk met feeble and doubtful response. Even his own son, Anson, demurred, and the fighting Teegre stood irresolute. Posey's first son, Jess, with the prisoners in Blanding. All the time Posey was trying to stir up the old Paiute fighting spirit, those terrible forty men kept coming straight up Mule Creek, closer and closer.

It was beyond belief! Forty men stringing along under that rock where the last dodging one of them could have been mowed down by the Paiute's big guns like rats in a trap. Loaded with arms in their impregnable defense the Paiutes stood without heart to fire a shot! The days of the big fights were no more. Hatch, Mike, Sanop, and their fellow-terrors lay mouldering lowly among the rocks. Their day was fled —Poke knew it—Posey was soon to find out.

The fighting Paiutes on the island rock stood in a trance. A spell! No heart to fight. No impetus to flee. And all the time those forty men rode steadily forward with grim and resolute purpose.

A squaw shrieked. The Mormons were riding right up the trail they had made the night before! The camp bolted instanter. Like a bunch of wild steers they scrambled off that campground in desperate confusion.

One man snatched a sack of flour and carried it in front of him on his pony, but others had all they

could do to get their children with them in their
saddles. They fled to the southwest, trampling the
brush and breaking the limbs of the trees. They left
the bread, half-cooked or burned, in dutch ovens by the
fire. They left pans, trinkets, charms, treasures, goats,
bedding.

General Posey watched the awful drama with
sinking heart. O the shameful, yellow streak in his
tribe! His people on whom he doted! He had never
been able to imagine anything so terrible— so de-
grading. The invincible spirit of old Paiutedom was
dead! Posey faced the fight alone. It was for him,
if possible, to save the last besmirched vestige of their
honor. He would at least cover their disgraceful retreat.

The desperate Paiutes took their horses down the
southwest side of the island, pushing them off, pulling
them off, any way to get them down fast, no matter if
it broke their legs or their necks. Posey maneuvered
around to watch the enemy. When some of them began
to circle the island on the south side, where they could
have headed off his people, Posey fired at them, ar-
resting their progress, that his white-feather tribe
might have time to escape. In this effort to save his
craven people, Posey was advertising his own position
to the posse. What the difference! What was there
left to live for now? If the posse failed to kill him, he
would die in the storm of that evil cloud which was
blowing in with a black roar from the horizon— the
sure fate of the bad-medicine man.

The main part of Black's men came straight up
the trail. Some of them stopped to refresh themselves
on the edible portions of the deserted breakfast, as
if it had been thoughtfully provided for them when
they were so hungry and cold. The boom of a big

gun brought them to the south rim. On the shelf below they saw Posey by his black mare.

He was under their guns; he knew it at once. His quick old eye and his even more quick instinct caught their silhouettes above him the instant they appeared. He knew their artillery would spit out death, immunity or not. Darting from the beloved black mare, he disappeared like a chipmunk among the rocks.

He was too quick for a shot, but they marked the direction and the place of his disappearance. They descended the hill in leaps and bounds—his capture was as good as accomplished. They found the black mare just as he had left her, the skin-em-all mare with the saddle still warm from his body, the best animal which he had ever known, and which he was never to see again.

Forty men hunted that hillside in every section of its extent for Posey. They called every member to the job and combed the whole region in every direction, taking the most careful scrutiny of every possible hiding place on the entire surface. They peered over and under ledges, and between rocks, and even among the limbs of the trees. They failed to find one trace or sign beyond the mare. So far as they could tell the old man had resolved himself into thin air and blown away. General Posey had outwitted forty eager men.

When the fleeing Paiutes got down from the butte they expected to have the posse treading on their heels. They racked their brains for some kind of offering to propitiate that posse. They left all six horses they had stolen from the Ruin Spring field. They tied a white rag to a high limb of a dry cedar as a token of their humble desire to surrender. They longed to plead for mercy if only they dared to face the invincible men whom they couldn't kill, but who could kill them.

When the posse, instead of jumping all over them as they had expected, delayed to search for Posey, the Paiutes, surprised and delighted to have time to get out of the way, hurried on in spite of their peace-offering and their white flag, getting as far away as the minutes would permit. With this new ray of hope they resolved they must escape: they could not endure the hazard, and more still, the shame of being captured.

While the daylight lasted they panted forward. Then they dragged themselves on and on into the night, urging and belaboring their weary ponies till they stopped on the brow of a high vertical cliff. Dead-tired from the toil and exposure of the previous night, their children crying for food and rest, they determined in spite of everything to descend in the darkness to the wild region below.

They would slide down on ropes over the perilous wall. No one would dare to follow them. They would hide among the brush and the rocks. In the caves of this deep canyon they would be as hard to find as fine beads in the sand.

They had to leave their horses and even their beloved yellow dogs. Nothing stopped them. They made torches of cedar bark to light the perilous wall lest they plunge headlong to death. Then they began slipping down on the ropes along the cold, hard surface. Chilled with visions of what would happen if they fell, they gripped the rope till it burned their hands raw. In their awful anxiety they scarcely felt the merciless sandstone scrub the skin from their knuckles.

In the middle of the process their over-wrought imaginations told them the light of their torches had attracted the posse. Quick panic seized on all those remaining at the top. Wild to escape capture they burned their hands and peeled their joints at a bloody rate in getting down to the bottom with lightning speed. Anson Posey stepped out of one of his new shoes and ventured no delay in turning around to get it.

When the last one reached the bottom with palpitating heart beat and all the babies and children had been duly accounted for, behold! that sack of flour, their only morsel of food, had been left on the top of the cliff.

On the steep, hillside at the base of the vertical rock, they groped their way down through tangles of brush and over big rocks in the darkness—anywhere to get away— any place to hide from Black's bullet-proof men. Just which way they would go, they didn't know— didn't care.

Finding a strange hole in the hillside they plunged into it as mice running from a cat. They crawled on their hands and knees thirty feet and came out again into the open. It would afford no shelter, but they followed their leader through it and went on.

No one slept a wink. No one rested. No one stopped. Reaching the bottom of the deep canyon, they started down along the dry creek-bed, only to change their minds and climb the west side to a rough shelf at the base of the cliff. Then they followed that narrow footing back up the canyon.

When daylight came, the leaders ordered each one to step in the track of the one just ahead of him. The whole wretched company toiled over awful rock and through jungles of serviceberry—leaving but one track behind!

As bright morning beamed down at them over the cliff from which they had descended in the darkness, they saw outlined against the sky on top of that cliff, the dread silhouettes of their pursuers looking off in the depths towards them. They stopped stark still like young partridges hiding. Those evil eyes on the high rim must not discover them. They lacked little of choking their babies to keep them quiet.

Their enemies had found the horses, the dogs, and even that precious sack of flour for lack of which these Paiutes felt their limbs growing weak and shaky. While every pair of black eyes among the brush on the hillside was staring with awe and dread at those forms on the lofty rim, one of the posse came forward with that sack of flour in his hands and emptied it in a great white cloud down the dizzy face of the towering rock. What could that mean? Something unrelenting and inexorable—starvation! Their precious flour scattered to the wind before their eyes.

Chilled with new alarm they sank slowly to the ground, toiling forward as before, only now they suffered the added torment of keeping out of sight. Mile after mile they crawled forward, their hands at their babies' throats lest the little ones utter a betraying cry. When they turned their ears with breathless hush to the wind, they caught echoes of the determined hunters behind them. Hunger gnawed at their vitals and sapped their strength.

Later in the afternoon they saw a place where they could cross the canyon on smooth rock without leaving any betraying track. Making sure that no one was within sight or hearing, they crossed to the east side. Near the top of that east wall, hidden well by trees and brush, they found a big cave with a seep of water in the back of it.

Staggering in on its sandy floor they sank exhausted, discouraged. Some of the squaws declared

they would go no farther. Then they all became quiet
and listened again—disturbing sounds came on the
breeze from the opposite rim. They began to build a
rude stone wall across the mouth of the cave, but when
it was three feet high they sank wearily on the sand
to rest, and no one ever proposed that they go on with
it.

At sundown they heard startling commotion immediately below their hangout. The squaws and the
children wept. They peered down among the trees for
what they might be able to see, while the men sat irresolute, climbing to the big guns which they had no
spirit to use.

"O let's surrender!" pleaded the squaws and the
papooses in despair.

"You surrender!" ordered Teegre bitterly. "We
can't."

Fear had frozen the very springs of their impulses.
Fear and shame. No enemy had ever followed them like
this before. Never before had they been powerless to
kill or to frighten their adversaries. The women
couldn't even find courage to go down and offer to
surrender. "They'll kill us on sight," they wailed.

Would the men of the posse shoot a child? No!
A child could go down in safety with a flag of sub-
mission. They fastened a white rag on a stick and gave
it to a twelve-year-old boy. "Tell them there is no one
here but women and children who will give up, if they
won't be sent to prison," Teegre ordered.

The boy trembled from head to foot. His knees
smote together but he descended the hill waving the
white emblem.

At the bottom he saw the terrible men of the posse.
Some of them had their guns ready to shoot as soon
as he came in sight. How could they know what to

expect from a white flag offered by the treacherous
Posey's people?

The little fellow staggered forward, his limbs and
facial muscles half palsied with fright.

"*Impo ashanty?*" (What do you want?) one of the
men asked.

"The squaws and papooses want to give up, if you
won't send them to prison," the boy managed to mutter.

"We promise nothing!" the same man growled in
Paiute. "If you don't come down, we'll climb the hill
and get every one of you."

Pale and with short catchy breath the boy climbed
back to the hangout. They listened in a hush to all he
said. The men had been ready to shoot him—they
were *tooitch to-buck* (heap mad) and they were going
to come right up.

What could they do? faint and famished and worn
to a frazzle. Since they couldn't fight they either must
choose death from starvation or trust themselves to
the mercy of their enemies. The men in the cave might
endure hunger indefinitely if by so doing they could
avoid capture, but the women and children had already
reached their limit.

"Go again," Teegre ordered. "They won't hurt you.
Tell them the men are all gone."

When the boy whimpered with fear, his mother
took the flag and went with him. "There are no men
with us," she declared as soon as she saw the stern
faces of the posse. "Only squaws and papooses. We'll
come down, if you won't send us to prison."

"You're a gang of infernal liars!" growled the
interpreter. "The men are there—we know it. Your
people started this fight, and we're going to follow you
up and get every last one."

The prospect looked gloomy when she reported to the hangout. Maybe one of the men could put up a better talk and save the others. The same squaw went again, Anson Posey with her. Nervous and trembling before these invincible men he insisted there was nobody on the hill above but women and children. He swore he had been out hunting and had just happened to find them there. The women wanted to surrender if they wouldn't have to go to the *calaboose* (jail).

"You are all blasted liars!" hissed the interpreter in disgust.

They held Anson prisoner and told the squaw to bring the others.

Night came on. Most of Black's men stood around a big fire, while others of their number took their horses down to Karnell's ranch for the night. The squaws and papooses came stringing down the hill, but only three of the men came. The others waited in shame and fear and uncertainty, clinging still to the guns which they were so strangely unable to use.

One of the men who had come down and surrendered, decided to dodge back among the shadows. Without a moment's hesitation, Lee Newman fired at him. The shot went wild and the fellow got away, but it gave the others a chilly acquaintance with the sternness of the hands into which they had fallen. No other one of them ventured to make a crooked move.

"Now look here," said Dave Black to Anson Posey next morning, "We know the other men are up there. You are to lead us to them. We'll follow behind you with our guns. If they fire on us, every one of us will shoot you in the back."

Anson started up the hill with six big guns all but punching him in the spine. He called loudly in his barbarous dialect to his friends, telling them to be mighty careful how they acted or he would be blown to ribbons. He told them to hide their big guns and come down some other way to the camp.

Finding the hangout empty, Black and his men returned with their one prisoner to camp only to find Teegre and his fellowfighters waiting there. They had arrived to surrender themselves with half a dozen guns of twenty-two calibre, declaring that was all the guns they had ever had with them.

"Where are your big guns?" Dave Black demanded.

O, they had just been out hunting rabbits and had no need for anything but the small guns. They had just happened to find the squaws and papooses there in the cave. They looked as innocent as angels and told their lies like experts.

Black returned with three men to the hangout, examining the network of tracks. They found where the Paiutes had buried an armful of big guns between two rocks. Going back down with all this heavy artillery, Black got just one quick glance from Teegre and his fellow liars before they riveted their eyes on the ground at their feet.

"No guns, hey?" Black chuckled, but the Paiutes had nothing to say. Not one of them raised his eyes. They were whipped—whipped to a frazzle on their own ground for the very first time in all their history.

"Now, where's Posey?" Black demanded. "Yes, you DO know where he is, and you better tell."

"No sabe," they repeated, shaking their heads. But they had a question of their own, a question to which they attached much importance: "How many Mormons got killed?" they asked eagerly.

At first they refused to believe that in all the shooting not one white man had been hurt. Then they talked earnestly and wound up with another question, "You, where's Posey?" The fact of the matter was that they were even more eager than Black to know what had become of the bad-medicine man who had got them into all this trouble.

The posse took the renegades like a herd of sheep down the canyon. The need for keeping the babies quiet by choking or otherwise having passed, the babies cried—the little folks cried— the squaws cried. The men of the posse took the smaller children with them on their horses. From Karnell's ranch they sent for trucks to come by Navaho Trail up the Comb and haul their prisoners down to the other Paiute prisoners who waited at a newly made bull pen in Blanding.

Chapter Twenty-five

AN OLD ACCOUNT CLOSED

This was the fifth day of the fight. News of it had found its way into big headlines in the newspapers on the outside, but no one from the outside had come to take over. The explosive situation, coming up so suddenly, had left the people of San Juan no alternative but to meet it themselves, in their own way, with understanding born of forty-three years of experience with the Paiutes.

The Mormons had raised a generation of men in San Juan who knew the rocks as well as the Paiute knew them. It became their duty to do what had been attempted in vain for the last forty-three years.

State and federal officers were due to arrive in Blanding that day, but it was too late for the new arrivals to cancel the wholesome lesson already delivered to the troublesome tribe. The Paiutes had learned more in the last five days than ever before in all their history.

While the latest round up of Paiutes waited at Karnell's ranch for the trucks, some of the squaws were allowed to go hunting for lost goats and other things left in the stampede from the island. It was not considered necessary to watch them or to take any precaution about their return, they would know when it was meal time, and after their starving experience, they wouldn't have been absent even for a horse.

Two squaws tracking goats southwest of the island, heard someone call from the cliff to the south. Climbing up they found Posey in a little cave near the top. He had been hiding there ever since he parted with his black mare. He drank from a little seep in the ledge and subsisted on what he had salvaged from that forsaken breakfast. He was too lame to move far from his hiding place, and he leaned heavily on a big stick.

He listened in torture to the account of the capture of his people. Dark, dark, prospect! Yet of the darkest phase of his predicament, the two women said nothing to him, though they talked of it with each other as they got out of his hearing. They could hardly wait to tell the men of the tribe what they wanted most of all to know: where to find Posey, the bad-medicine man.

The trucks came sputtering up the sandy wagon tracks and took all the Paiutes away, leaving the region empty and silent. No one was staying at Karnell's ranch. No human being, red or white, lingered between Posey and his far-flung circle of ragged horizon. Aside from the plaintive cry of cedarbirds, winging their way at wide intervals over his solitude, he heard only the moaning of the wind through the trees and over the cliff-brow above him. He heard it every day. He heard it still when he listened for sounds in the night.

When those truckloads of renegades reached Blanding, they joined the rest of their people in the bull pen surrounded by armed guards. Inside that closely-built barbwire fence, eight feet high, they could indulge as much pride and self-esteem as a herd of steers in a corral. No such humiliating come-down had ever been known to them nor to any of their ancestors.

News of Posey's whereabouts went through the tribe like water into a dry sponge. They discussed it in their fifty-mile ride in the trucks. They told it to their people in the bull pen. They had it on their tongues and in their cryptic idiom, even though they swore in pidgin English with the next breath that they had no idea what had become of their leader.

The second wife and the two grown sons heard the murmurs of angry blame from the tribe. Posey by his insistent cajolery had wheedled them into the most distressing and humiliating experience of their history. He had made more bad medicine than Bridger Jack, Kane, and all the other bad-medicine men together.

Not only had he led them to defeat and disaster, but his extra bad medicine had cast over them a devilish spell which rendered them powerless to shoot straight, and finally powerless to shoot at all. If ever they got their freedom, Posey would pay the price for all this evil. Possibly he would starve to death or die of his wounds before they could reach him. Let him die!

That little hand-sized cloud had come in, big and black and bristling with lightning from the distance, but Posey could not hear its thunder or see the depth of its gloom. He lived his wretched hours of fear and trembling waiting for dangers far removed and never to come to him.

The second wife, pretending to be annoyed at not being allowed to hunt goats south of the island, contended that she had lost a valuable milch doe. Thus she obtained permission and a horse to go hunting. She went straight to her ill-fated lord in his solitude. She left with him the little sack of grub brought along for her dinner and she didn't by any means fail to remind him that his disaster was the result of his failing to listen when she wanted him to wait for her invincible brother. But she did fail, as no true friend would have done, to tell him about the rising and murderous cry against him from his own people. She failed also to make any plan or effort to save him from the wounds which were eating his life away. She kept his condition a secret from the people of Blanding who, if they had known it, would have made every necessary effort to save him. She had no thought of nursing him to health as Toorah would have done at the peril of her life.

Instead, the second wife left him there alone, clinging to his guns in fear of being found by white men. She knew that his great danger was from his own people and his wounds, and that if one failed to get him the other would unless someone reached out to save him.

Posey's sons also got permission to hunt, and they left food and blankets at his cave. But they told the old sufferer nothing of what was brewing against him. They dared not to brave the popular tribal curse against the bad medicine man. Not even Scotty, his brother, did anything to save him, nor dropped the faintest hint to the Mormons of how he lay dying.

If the dead Toorah had been on the scene, she would have made her way to that cave, even if she had been compelled to do it in the night with her wrists tied. She would have fought his enemies even if they were her own brothers. And she would have nursed him back to health at the peril of her own life.

The old Paiute law knew no mercy, not for the very best man ever born among them. If it were Posey to transgress their law, the penalty was exactly what it had ever been—death.

The matter of his witchcraft and the place of his exile were tribal secrets. Anyone revealing them would be a traitor. During the better part of a month while the Paiutes waited in their bull pen for Uncle Sam's verdict, Posey's wife and sons and brother maintained their silence along with the rest of the tribe. Full well they knew that their loved one lay suffering with an ugly wound, alone in the solitude. If he survived, it would be to meet a disgraceful death at the hands of his people. Possibly, his family hoped he would expire in honor there alone at his hideout.

When Posey first took refuge in the cave, he preserved a constant vigil lest he be surprised by men of the posse. He held to his gun every hour of the day and night. He lay between two great rocks for hours and hours at a time, scanning the country around the mouth of Mule Creek. The plain imprint of his weary old limbs could be seen there for months afterward.

After their few short visits, his sons came no more. No one came—not even the second wife to tell him why he was in such a sorry mess. Fearful and apprehensive at first that someone would find him, Posey began to be equally fearful that no one would find him. At first he refrained from making a fire lest the smoke should advertise his hiding place, but later he longed to see anybody, red or white.

By painful effort he climbed to the top of the rim above his cave. There in the open space he lighted signal fires—signals of distress. During the long hours while the spring winds moaned through the cedars, he made these fires to give out their smoke by day and their light by night that any hunter or wanderer might be guided to him in his distress.

As weeks dragged on he reduced his daily allowance of food, for at the end of his limited supply he saw the dark spectre of starvation, even if he should survive his wounds. He poulticed those wounds with soft pine gum, for although they had healed on the surface, he had torturing pus-pockets on the bone.

In his silent world of agony Posey saw starvation and disease fighting with each other to claim him. He toiled back and forth from his spring in the cave to his signal fires on top, feeding his fires and praying that their smudge or their gleam would bring some-one to deliver him from the monster whose teeth sank deeper into his vitals every day. These signals were his prayers to all the world for help. His people knew he was here in great distress—why didn't they come?

On a little elevation up there among his fires he improvised a seat accommodated to his wounded body. There he could watch the distance for any indication of life. All around that seat, as far as his arm could reach while he sat, he smoothed the earth with his heavy stick, patting and rubbing and scratching the cold sand to relieve the anguish of his monotony. That mute record, made by his untrained hand which could not write a word, told his story in eloquent pleading a long time after the old stick had fallen from his palsied fingers.

In that little area on top the rock above his cave, he burned everything available for his fires and his smudges. He made fires in thirty places. And what did it bring!

Two Paiutes had married out of the tribe and brought their consorts home. A squaw had married a Navaho man, and a Paiute man had married a Na-vaho squaw. It resulted in a leak of tribal secrets, for although the Mormons got no enlightenment thus far from anybody about what had become of Posey, it was whispered among the Navahos that he was a bad-medicine man. He had cast an evil spell over his people and brought them to shame and disaster. They had deserted him to die alone in the hills west of Comb

Wash. The report traveled from hogan to hogan and camp to camp.

Then away off there on the boundary of the reservation, away there where the dry water-course of the Comb Wash joins with the San Juan River, a Navaho came riding to the Rincone Ford. He was a big man with a foolish little greasy hat strapped over his grizzled hair. He rode fast with raised quirt, and he gazed eagerly towards the Elk Mountain ahead.

In the upper valley of the Comb he scanned the hills to the west as he rode, till he discerned a rising smoke from the high rim. *"Ouh, nishi-e!"* (Yes, I see it!) he purred to himself with great satisfaction. Laying the quirt along his horse's thigh he quickened his trot into the mouth of Mule Creek. On he hurried, guided by that smoke on the lofty rim. Under his left arm he carried a Colt automatic pistol, a trick he had learned in a card game at the big *yabetchi* (festival). Also he carried an ugly dent in his left cheek.

With nervous fingers he urged his pony to a lope while he reviewed the program he had been framing for two days past. No act from under cover would appease his fierce craving—they must stand again face to face as they had stood by the black mare after that big *ducki*.

When the skunk looked up with a hateful snarl, "Coyote!" he would answer it with, "Pu-neeh!" And at that supreme moment of sweet revenge, he would put on the skunk's face the same kind of mark he had carried in his own cheek since the big *yabetchi*.

Then the coyote would hurry away with raised quirt, leaving the skunk dazed and outraged to endure the miserable little bit of life still remaining for him in his wretched struggle. There would be no last word. No report of their meeting.

The coyote came down from that rim exactly as he had planned, leaving anguish and consternation behind. With raised quirt he rode back down the Comb and crossed Rincone Ford into the reservation.

To assuage the agony of that savage dent in his cheek, Posey, half blind with pain and crazed with anger, made a poultice of the little flour still remaining. He bound it with shaking fingers on his bursting face. He started for the seep to cool his parched tongue, but sank in a stupor and never regained understanding of the mad world around him.

After weeks had passed—ample time for a wounded man, neglected and alone, to die from his injuries—Posey's sons got permission to hunt again. They brought back word that their father was dead. They had buried him where they found him.

Men who had taken part in the fight and who had been perplexed at Posey's mysterious disappearance, followed his sons tracks back to their father's grave. Removing the shallow covering they lifted the poor old corpse out into the light of day.

It was Posey. No possibility of these men being mistaken. They had known him many years. They looked him over carefully, found the two bullet-wounds in his hip, and knew when and how he got them.

But that poultice of hard dough on his face? They removed it and saw the bloody imprint of a hard blow as from a gun-barrel. They took pictures of his poor dead features, but could only guess the real tragedy of that last bitter day.